THE LEXONITE LEGACY

THE DRAGON STONE

C. N. STRAUSER

Cover illustration by
JACOB CHAVEZ

C.N. STRAUSER

This book is a work of fiction. Names, characters, places, and incidents are the product of the author's imagination or are used fictitiously. Any resemblance to actual events, locales, or persons, living or dead, is coincidental.

This book is dedicated to my family but especially to my departed brother Vincent, and to my departed sister-in-law, Robin, who will always be in our hearts and greatly missed until we see each other again, singing with the angels.

1

"What is that disgusting smell?" Candade, wrinkling her nose, shook her head from side to side; unsuccessfully, she searched to find the source of the awful stench in order to rid herself of it. A sensation nudged at her memory… where had she smelled that before? Was it in the whispering forest? She just couldn't remember, but the acerbic smell seemed to follow her everywhere.

Candade sighed in defeat, and shook her head again to focus. Briefly, she glanced at the majestic dragon cliffs in the north. Its incredible beauty always calmed her nerves. Then she drew in one more deep breath and turned to the spectacular pistachio green, cacao-powered dragon lying in front of her.

"Swish," she asked her dragon, "what is wrong with you? That is the second time today that you snapped at me." She was extremely worried about him. Ever since the evil King Sanchezo kidnapped them, Swish didn't seem the same. He glared at her with one massive eye when he saw that she had moved closer to him while still sniffing. He knew what she was thinking.

You can sniff somewhere else because it ***isn't*** *me, and nothing is wrong with me. I would just like to sleep and you are bothering me.* Even in mind-speak, she felt Swish's low growl. He grumpily curled into a tight ball, swishing his tail over his humongous head to ignore her more thoroughly.

"Then why, when we were doing drills earlier today, did you lose focus?" she asked, while stepping back with a shake of her head, her brunette hair, cut short for dragon flying, barely disturbed. "We were supposed to maintain dragon formation and then do a synchronized roll immediately to our right around Cleto's dragon. We were supposed to be teaching him how to do it! Instead, when you fell out of formation before rolling, we looked as green as they get. Greecher was furious at us. He thought we were messing around."

Candade wasn't thrilled either. She knew that the dragon rider trainer was upset with them, which meant that he would give them the hardest jobs in the village to make up for the mistakes that they had made flying today or more accurately… he would give ***her*** the hardest jobs. Punishing Candade was supposed to be punishment enough for both her and her dragon because of the close bond that they had, but she really doubted that it bothered Swish that much, especially considering that he didn't look very bothered now while she was admonishing him. In fact, all he did was to feign a close snap at her to remind her that he was the dragon and she was a mere human.

She tried again, "As one of the more experienced riders and dragons flying in the festival, we should instruct the others, and look splendid in the process. We should be hearing a bunch of 'oohs' and 'awws' from our admirers in the village below, not 'hey watch out' and laughing."

After all, Candade and Swish had a reputation to uphold. They were known for the extraordinary tricks they performed when flying, and they couldn't even perform in a simple dragon formation today where a lead flyer represents the head and is followed by four flyers representing the wings and then a single file of flyers behind to represent the tail; it was meant to replicate one big dragon. "Greecher expects us to teach the younger riders, not to look confused and misguided doing a simple drill."

After saying a quick, *You're exaggerating*, in mind-speak and giving a look that implied she was pestering him, Swish refused to answer her further. Instead, he buried his head deeper into his tail.

Something was wrong, and he refused to talk about it or to go to the healers with her. She just didn't know what to do, and a vague uneasiness plagued her relentlessly, making it hard for her to relax.

In a few days' time, they were supposed to fly in the Mermival, a village celebration for the return of the contenders from the Primitus, which was the first challenge of the choosing ceremony that allowed the Lexonite villagers to bond with a dragon. Yet Swish was in no way acting like himself, and they definitely were not prepared for the mock battle maneuvers that were supposed to be the culminating event and the highlight of the evening.

Candade had actually been excited to perform this year since two of her friends, Nohmran and Lisbeth, were contenders in this year's Primitus ceremony. If they were successful and beat the other challengers in this Primitus, then they would get the chance to do the Secundus challenge and climb the dragon cliffs to bond with a dragon egg. She was hoping they were successful. She owed them a lot since they had rescued her from the evil King Sanchezo last year when he had kidnapped her and tortured her. She shivered just remembering it and rubbed the pain she sometimes still felt in her wrist. It didn't help that she knew he was still out there somewhere.

Staring at her dragon, she reminisced about how the

village healers said that she was healed. She didn't feel healed. She still felt the pain; so she decided on her own to go to the herbalist. Though the herbs she got from him didn't seem to help anymore at all either. Indeed, Candade recognized that even now she and Swish were not back to normal in either body or spirit. As if to confirm this, Swish still hadn't even bothered to really answer her, which left Candade even more frustrated with her dragon.

Looking at him now, she wondered if her connection to Swish transferred her uneasy feelings to him even as he slept, since she heard him angrily growling in his sleep. His leg also twitched and jerked erratically. She knew their bond connected them, so maybe it was possible that her upset feelings were conveyed to him. She had to try to stop worrying. It wasn't healthy for either of them. She sighed and moved to sit down under a tree a few feet away from him as she watched him. Swish had told her once that dragons rarely dreamed, but he sure did look like he was in the middle of a nightmare right now. It was almost as if he was battling something unseen even as he slept.

Glancing into the sky over her sleeping dragon, she noticed that several wild dragons were now flying over the imposing dragon cliffs. It seemed they watched their eggs more vigilantly now since the evil king had murdered her brother and stolen an egg. *Oh, dragons value their young, maybe even more than humans do*, she thought. *Maybe that is why our world is such a mess... we don't guard and value our offspring enough... in the "shell" or out of the "shell". Failing to recognize the importance of all humanity, we end up warring amongst ourselves. I sometimes wonder why the dragons even bother with us. At any rate, I doubt they have to worry about their young being stolen again. Even Sanchezo knew better than to steal an unbonded egg with the number of wild dragons that would fly in to protect it. That is why he went after a dragon egg that had already been bonded to a villager. He had his henchman, Taylor, murder the baby dragon's human bond, and then he forced a magical connection between them with dark magic, something the elders explained he could only do once Taylor had made the choice to accept the evil path.*

She had a tear in her eye as she remembered losing her brother in the previous year's challenge. Her pondering was interrupted when she heard the crunching of leaves behind her as someone approached. "Hey, Lea," she said without even turning around.

"How did you know it was me?" Lea pouted. She was disappointed that her sneaking skills were not up to par like she thought they were. Hopel's little sister had decided to follow Candade around "to help her" ever since Hopel had left on assignment. She would have recognized her approach anywhere.

"Well, you aren't as quiet as you think you are for one thing," she replied. "You need to walk on the balls of your feet and try to stay on the grass and out of the leaves."

"I guess," Lea replied, tossing her long charcoal black hair out of her eyes and scrunching up her nose. "What are you doing here anyway?"

"Well right now, I'm sitting here watching the dragons flying over the dragon cliffs and wondering why they bother with us and our warring ways," she replied sullenly.

"Well, that is easy to know," Lea lifted her right eyebrow as if annoyed that Candade didn't know the obvious answer and replied, one hand on her hip. "The High God gave them to us to help us and vice versa. Everyone knows that." After everything that Candade went through, Lea knew she needed a friend right now, especially since all of Candade's friends were away, which is why she stayed near her. Before he left, Nohm, her brother's friend, made her promise. He also made Lea promise not to tell Candy, which is what everyone affectionately called her. Watching her friend now, she didn't think she was looking that well, short hair matted to her head, and skin paler than usual, she looked depleted. Briefly, she thought that if she ever became a dragon rider, she would tie her hair up before she would ever cut it short like Candade did.

"Okay, squirt. You, no doubt, are right." Candade smiled. She knew Lea really admired her, so if she said anything that disappointed her, it was quite evident in the way Lea reacted. *If only I were more patient*, she thought. Out loud she began, "Hey, how about…"

Before she could say anything further, Swish startled both of them. Roaring, Swish abruptly raised his head and fiercely growled into the air as if he was battling something unseen. Shocked, Candade went to grab her sword before she realized that she wasn't wearing it. Looking around frantically, she was unable to see anything that would have angered him. Then suddenly, with another mighty roar, he lunged himself into the air, his tail almost swiping the girls in his haste. "Hey," Lea cried out and they both jumped up off the ground to avoid being whacked with his tail.

Candade, still panicked and disoriented by his actions, screamed into the air, "Hey watch out, Swish… what is going on?" "Where are you going?"

To Candade's dismay, Swish didn't answer her. He flew off into the sky until only a speck of visible tail remained and even that was quickly gone. This had never happened before. Swish may have left her for various dragon reasons previously, but never would he have closed off his mind to her and refused to communicate with her like this, nor would he have taken off so abruptly. Candade was bewildered and unable to move physically, though her thoughts scattered in all directions. First, the relentless smell that wouldn't leave her still plagued her so that even in the midst of the commotion one of her first thoughts was that he had been right… the smell wasn't from him… only to be followed by a torrential bombarding of thoughts related to concern for him. Both girls stood there blankly, shielding their eyes, and staring into the now empty sky.

2

An explosion so loud that it sounded only seconds away, Nohmran and Lisbeth searched for the streak of light that would indicate how close the lightning really was to them. *Too close*, Nohmran thought as he motioned to his cousin, Lisbeth. It was hard to see through the hailstorm, and there was no place to get cover. Thus, they had no choice but to keep moving, storm or no storm.

The Lexonite teenagers were deep into the Whispering Forest, struggling to make it through their first challenge. The cousins, who were also very good friends, had decided to do the challenge together this year. Hopel, a friend of both of theirs from the time they all were young children, had tried to prepare them since he had already bonded in the fore year and made it through all of the challenges. He had told them how difficult and dangerous his time in the forest was, and that was considering he was lucky enough to have good weather and not this mess that they were stuck in. Still, if they only had to endure bad weather they were thankful. They knew Hopel had run into a Miaciartk, a creature that Hopel had described as looking like it was half bear and half wolf because he wasn't familiar with the creature, so it wasn't easy for him to describe it. They couldn't imagine dealing with that and this pelting rain. They weren't keen on running into any wild animals in this muddy mess. They didn't think they would be able to fight or run very well.

Hopel and their other friend, Cleto, who also bonded last year, had been lucky to escape the Miaciartk. They are deadly creatures, especially when hungry. Now, with all the spooky sounds the cousins heard and the torrential rain, they had little doubt as to how the forest got its name, and they were only hoping that they didn't run into any creatures like the Miaciartk.

At least they had Hopel's advice to draw upon, and another advantage for them was that Nohmran had the fortune of being tutored by his uncle, Xian, on what to expect in this unusual forest. His Uncle Xian was a healer and his work required that he explore lands that many people didn't venture out into, places that included this forest. The healers needed to seek herbs in these distant places for various medicines that they used in conjunction with dragon magic to heal both dragons and humans, and this need for herbs afforded Nohmran a good education from his uncle's experiences in the Whispering Forest.

Unfortunately, his uncle could not prepare him for this weather. The thunderstorm that was raging overhead was literally shaking the earth beneath them. Nohmran was shouting something at the top of his lungs, but they couldn't hear each other over the deafening thunder. Every time another bolt of lightning zigzagged through the sky, Lisbeth ducked as if to escape it, feeling as if she was about to get zapped at any minute.

Nohmran decided to resort to pointing to the only place that he could see to run for cover and hoped that Lisbeth understood his meaning. He took off running towards a small rocky hill which he had finally spotted. An ensemble of rocks and fallen trees protruded out over the top of it in such a manner that they could crouch under it to give them a little shelter. There weren't many mountainous areas in this forest, so he considered himself lucky that he had spotted this ledge. He was only a few feet into his sprint when he felt something grab his ankle. He couldn't move! Something yanked him down to the ground, and his entire foot sank beneath the mud. "Lisbeth, waaait," he yelled out. "I'm stuck. Something's got me."

Unfortunately the ear-piercing thunder crashed so loudly that Lisbeth wasn't able to hear him. It wasn't until Lisbeth had almost reached the ledge that she realized he wasn't behind her. "Nohm, Nohm," she shouted her cousin's nickname, but got no response. She wasn't sure what she should do. It was even harder to see now. With the rain pouring down in torrents, she was only able to discern a few feet in front of her. Even the unusual red hair that the cousins shared wouldn't help them to find each other in this mess. *Oh great,* she thought, *the last thing I want to do is get split up in this crazy forest. We'll be lucky if we find each other again before we get back.* She put her arms out in front of her to avoid running into anything and started to carefully backtrack, continuing to call out his name until she finally heard him calling her too. When she eventually reached him, he was shouting and pointing to his foot, and she realized that he couldn't move. She felt beneath the mud for his foot and tried to move the boughs that gripped him. "Calm down," she shouted. "It's only a branch." Another thunderous roar shook the earth, and the fossilized finger-like branches ensnared him further and refused to budge. The more he yanked on his foot, the tighter it seemed to trap him.

"That's no ordinary branch," he yelled back.

"Overreact much? Stop moving. You are making it worse," she replied, still shouting at the top of her lungs.

Nohmran's shifting weight was causing him to sink deeper into the sludge, making it feel as if he had a ton of weight on his foot, and if he sunk any deeper, he would be unable to move at all.

After calming down a little, he realized that he and his cousin were soaked and that she was probably right, and he was over-reacting to the branch. "You can go get under cover. I'll get loose eventually and catch up with you," he shouted.

"Well it may only be a branch, but I'm not going without you," his red-headed cousin screamed back stubbornly, while shaking her head no. "We don't need to get split up in this mess. When I count to three, we will both pull at the same time. Hold on though. I want to try cutting through it first." She wasn't sure if he heard her words or understood her hand motions, but she thought he was getting the gist of it. She felt for the branches beneath the mud and with her knife in her right hand, she cut and sliced at the branches while being careful to avoid her cousin's foot.

She was cutting through the first branch when a blast of air whirled up the boughs of the nearest tree, probably the one that she was cutting through, and with a gust, the wind appeared to move the branch, which slapped her on the side of her head and knocked her down. "Ow," she yelled as she got back up and started yanking more frantically at her cousin's foot. *Did that tree just whack me on purpose?*

Even if it was just in her imagination that the tree intentionally smacked her, she didn't want to try to cut it again. "No more cutting," she yelled. "On the count of three, we will both pull. One, two, three, pull." While Nohmran yanked at his foot, she yanked at the branches, pulling them away from him. She wasn't sure which action caused the branches to loosen, but finally, his foot came free, and they raced for the protruding ledge, trying not to trip on the plethora of vines that were barely visible and still seemed to be grabbing at them both.

It seemed like it took hours to arrive at the ledge because the wind certainly wasn't cooperating with their efforts to reach a drier area in this crazy forest. In fact, it seemed to purposefully push them back two steps for every one that they took forward, but eventually they reached the overhanging growth.

Unfortunately, they both realized pretty quickly that they were still going to get wet with the way the wind continued to slam the rain into them as if it were still trying to seek revenge for Lisbeth's earlier offense against the trees.

Lisbeth glanced around her nervously. "Are you sure those rocks and that tree is going to hold?" Lisbeth asked. "We are getting wet anyway, so I would rather stay in the storm and get wetter than get crushed."

"I think that growth has been there for centuries. I'm pretty sure we are all right and being out there is way worse than it is here," he replied.

Lisbeth wavered for a few minutes more before finally following him completely under the overgrowth.

Afterwards, they didn't attempt to talk further. They pressed their backs against the rock wall and waited for the storm to abate.

The next morning the cousins started out again, walking in the direction of the field where they could obtain the magical feathers they needed for the choosing ceremony. The feathers could only be found in the Strawthorn Field, and Hopel had told them a strategy to get them with the least amount of danger.

As they were hiking along, Lisbeth got the strange sensation that they were being followed. She turned around a few times and thought she saw something, but then determined it must only be the shadows. Once, she even thought she spotted a dark, shadowy shape with glowing eyes staring at her. "Did you see that?" she asked Nohm.

He looked around. "See what?"

Glancing around in every direction, she didn't see it again. "Uh, nothing, I guess." This forest tended to make her imagination intensify, not necessarily in the best creative direction, so she again decided it must be the shadows.

At one point when the feeling of being followed was just too much for her, she grabbed her cousin's arm to stop him and gestured for him to hide with her behind a rock. They had been through too much over the past year to not be of a suspicious, cautious nature after one of their friends had been kidnapped and another one murdered.

Slowly, a girl who looked about a year younger than Lisbeth came into view and approached near them. She stopped and looked around, apparently confused that she could no longer hear them ahead of her. Lisbeth vaulted out from behind the rock, "Aha! Why are you following us?"

The girl, frightened, jumped at first, but then on realizing that they had been hiding behind the big rock, her face grew red and she angrily screamed, "Hey… what are you doing scaring me like that?"

"You answer my question first!" Lisbeth countered threateningly. "Why are you following us? You could have told us that you were behind us at any time."

"Uh, who said I was following you. We are going in the same direction." She retorted irritably.

"I know you. You are the girl who moved to the village two years ago… Courtnia, right?"

"Yeah, so?" She snarled back at them. Courtnia was tired of people saying she wasn't a Lexonite and shouldn't try the challenge. "My mom is a Lexonite, which makes me one too, and I have a right to try the challenge."

"Whoa there," Nohmran interrupted the girls. "Who said anything about you not having a right to be here? We were just wondering why you were following us when you could have just said something. It is a little unnerving you know… to be followed."

"Again, we are going in the same direction," she snapped. "I'm not following you. If you don't like it… too bad."

"Well, you should have at least asked to join us since you were right behind us," Lisbeth shot back.

"If I wanted to join you, I guess I would have asked," Courtnia growled.

This Courtnia girl has too much attitude, Nohmran thought. *Could be trouble.* Out loud, before Lisbeth could reply, he said, " At any rate, I don't want anyone *following* us and scaring me out of my wits, intentional or unintentional, and since you are here now, we might as well work together."

"What…" Lisbeth started to protest but stopped when Nohmran shook his head at her. "Fine, she can join us, but she better leave her attitude here."

"You're assuming that I want to join you. I just said that I didn't."

"Look, it is up to you, but I don't see why we shouldn't work together since you are here. This forest can be dangerous," Nohm replied in a calming voice.

"Fine, for now… but I will do what I need to do to be one of the first five and win this thing," Courtnia said as she pushed ahead of them.

Nohm just sighed and followed her while Lisbeth glared at him.

After a few minutes of walking, the feeling that they were being watched had not subsided. Even though Courtnia had now joined them and the three youths were walking together, Lisbeth still couldn't shake the feeling that someone or something was watching them.

The rain hadn't returned, but neither had the sunstar. There was a pleasant earthy aroma following the rain that would be calming and pleasing except that there was also a chill in the air, which was accompanied by darkness everywhere. The gray clouds above barely let any sunstar light through the thick canopy of branches. Courtnia noticed the sunstar light that did make it through the branches seemed to barely make it past the boughs it reached before it was overcome by the darkness again.

She had been hiking with Nohm and Lisbeth for a few hours already, and was thoroughly glad that her leather boots and wool breeches were standing up to the dense, thorny brush and shrubs in this forest. Dragon riders and any females that wanted to be dragon riders did not wear dresses, and Courtnia would have no time for such silliness even if it was practical, and it most certainly was not practical.

Whenever Nohm or Lisbeth tried to speak to her, she responded abruptly with one word answers only. After all, she didn't join them for the conversation or the company, and after they found the field, she didn't think that she would need their help any more for anything, and she meant what she said when she told them she planned to be one of the winners. They had no idea what it had taken for her to get here, and she had done it on her own without anyone's help. The Lexonite Council almost wasn't going to let her even try the challenge because they said that she wasn't born in the village, even though her mother was from Lexonite. Then finally, they decided that the dragons could choose or not choose her for themselves if she even made it to the cliffs. It was rumored that the council had had second thoughts with another person in the fore year, but then they let him try the challenge, and he did bond. She was relieved that they gave her the same chance too. Her mother definitely didn't help her. For some reason, she didn't want her doing it… and forget her father, if you could even call him that.

She remembered her life back in Miflinsbine where they lived before moving to Lexonite. Her father popped in and out of their lives periodically, but when he was there, he was always putting her down and hurting her mother. She hated him. The last time he disappeared, she and her mother took off for the Lexonite village where her mother had a family to help them. If she had a dragon to protect them though, she wouldn't have to worry about him again. She couldn't understand why her mother didn't understand that, especially since he had broken her mother's arm once, and punched Courtnia in the stomach when he thought what she was doing wasn't good enough. One of her fears was that her father would find them and attack them again… maybe even killing them this time. She still could remember, like it happened just yesterday, her father's rampages. He would constantly call them names, only acting nice when he was trying to get something or pretend to their neighbors. At any rate, she didn't have to worry about him again. She shook her head as if trying to clear the memories out of it. She tried to focus her thoughts on the present hike towards the field, which was probably a good idea anyway because they had to be careful where they walked with all the thorns, large branches, and stones to avoid.

As she walked, she listened to Nohmran's and Lisbeth's chatter. They certainly didn't seem to have a care in the world. *It is so unfair*, she thought, *how easy some people's lives are.* At least they finally seemed to give up on getting her to talk to them and just left her alone. She sniffed and tossed her head. She gave up a long time ago caring what people thought about her. Growing up, she was teased constantly by the other kids in the village for her looks and because her family was poorer than most of the other villagers. Big boned, light brown hair and freckles, she wasn't pretty, so the other kids were constantly mean to her and the boys thought they could tease her incessantly about her looks and weight. A few of them quit after she beat them up though. She remembered how she used to dream of growing up and becoming beautiful. She scoffed at her younger self for caring about what they thought and allowing them to make her feel inferior… as if she somehow wasn't good enough for them because she wasn't pretty enough or rich enough. It was different in Lexonite. How much money someone had didn't really matter. It was more about having a dragon. That is what people respected. She would not let anyone tear her down anymore. She could and would become the best dragon rider out there, and she would help others in a way that she was never helped.

"Courtnia, Courtnia, will you snap out of it and listen?" Lisbeth's voice broke into her thoughts as she repeatedly tried to get her attention. "We are coming up on the field ahead. You have to be careful because the rose-thorn plant where the birds feed is deadly. Believe it or not, the plant will seem to call you and beckon to you in order to tempt you into the field, but don't get near it because one prick and you'll be dead. We have to keep our distance. We'll use these arrows with the string attached to them to hit one of the birds and then we'll pull it back without ever needing to get close. There will be enough feathers for all three of us. Our friend Hopel told us that this is how he and Cleto did it."

"Thanks anyway, I have my own way of doing it, and if it works I'll share *my* feathers with *you*," she curtly responded. Their eyes grew big as she pulled out what looked like a long eighteen-foot whip with a double-edged blade at the end of it. Another curved blade was also attached near the hilt at a fifty-degree angle. "I've been training with the dagger whip my whole life. Most people in my old village did." As if to prove her point, she somehow flung it off her neck to do a reverse spin and then off her elbow to face it in the other direction. With a final swish, she moved the whip in one fluid movement, crossing it in front of her like an x.

"Show off," Lisbeth muttered.

"Okay, well *that* is cool," Nohmran replied, "but I don't know if the whip is long enough to keep you far enough from the field."

"I'll manage," she responded abruptly again as she walked in front of them, ending the conversation.

"We better keep an eye on her," Nohmran told Lisbeth.

"I don't think she wants us to," Lisbeth answered, flipping her long red braid over her shoulder, "but I guess we will do it anyway."

"It's odd, but I still get the sense that we are being followed, and it can't be Courtnia since she is here with us now. Did you notice anything?" Nohmran whispered, not wanting anyone to hear him if they were still being followed.

"No, but I've had the same feeling for a while now. I didn't tell you because I thought it was just me. Plus, I think this forest is so spooky, you always feel like something or someone is watching you." Lisbeth shivered as she said it.

They saw the field ahead and were surprised at its beauty. Hopel's description didn't even come close to describing the plush red, purple, and pink roses that flooded the field, exuding a smell so tantalizing that if they didn't remind each other how deadly the roses really were, they would get too close to ever escape its trap. At the outer edge of the field, they began to hear the whispers that Hopel told them about. Sure enough it sounded like they were being enticed to get as close as possible. It sounded like the whispers were telling them to come hither, and eat of the sublime roses. Then again, they could be imagining it, and it could just be the sounds of the plush grass weeds brushing against each other. *No, it is real* Nohmran thought. *The first way to get you is to deceive you and make you believe something true really isn't.* "Just remember not to listen and to keep talking," Nohmran told his cousin. "Courtnia, you okay up there? Don't listen to the whispers no matter what," he yelled up to her.

Courtnia didn't respond, and she wasn't swinging her whip any longer. "This is what I was afraid of," Nohmran yelled as he rushed forward and grabbed her shoulders to pull her back.

"Hey, why'd you do that? I was okay," she snapped at him.

"Maybe so, but I think we should stay together and keep talking to each other to avoid getting hypnotized by the field," he answered.

Courtnia shrugged her shoulders, but she didn't refuse.

Shoulder to shoulder, the three of them kept talking, while they approached the field slowly, trying to spot one of the magical birds that sported the feathers they needed for the choosing ceremony. Courtnia even joined in to stay distracted. It was mostly nonsensical stuff about home and the other villagers, but it was working. They were able to ignore the sounds the strange flowers seemed to exude.

"There, I see one," Lisbeth whispered, noticing a beautiful bird with bright violet and cobalt plumage… *and was that fish scales underneath its feathers on its belly? Crazy, it was almost as if the legend was true. Surely a bird couldn't really be a fish that turned into a bird in order to eat something besides what fish eat?* She began to pull her bow and arrow out of its quiver.

"Hold on. I got this," Courtnia told her. Lisbeth looked startled and annoyed, but before she could say anything, Courtnia began swinging the whip over her head as she stepped forward and then with one swift forward motion, she flung it at the flying bird. She grunted when it didn't spear the bird, but knocked it to the ground instead— where it started limping towards the field. If it reached the roses, it would disappear from sight, and Lisbeth would feel horrible for the waste. At that moment, Lisbeth's arrow shot true. Whizzing through the air, it streaked in one direct path and penetrated the bird, which fell dead. Using the attached rope, she pulled it back to them.

"Well, that is good teamwork, I'd say," Nohmran told them both. "See, you can do anything with teamwork."

"Yeah, if you can find a good team," Lisbeth muttered.

"I didn't ask for help," Courtnia countered.

"See what I mean. That is appreciation for you. I was just surprised you even hit it with that thing, but unless you didn't notice… it was getting away," Lisbeth retorted.

"You both got it, okay, and arguing isn't helping us do anything but waste time. Now let's get out of here before we can't get out of here. Remember, we need to get going to be one of the first five challengers back to the village. If we aren't in the first five then we won't even have a chance at the dragon cliffs, and these feathers won't even matter," Nohmran said while shaking his head irritably and urging them forward after he plucked off some of the feathers. They each tucked a couple of the magical feathers away carefully in their pouches.

3

Hopel sat wondering how his friends were doing on their first challenge. He remembered doing his challenges last year. Thankfully, he now had his best friend as a result of those challenges, he thought, as he stared at his emerald and black dragon while they rested on the cliff, her enormous wings folded in around her while she slept. Hopel sat as near to her as possible in order to enjoy the heat that radiated off of her. They had decided to keep calling her Little One even though she was as gigantic as any dragon now. When he found out that they would choose a name for her together during her first year, he suggested name after name for her, but she just never liked any of the names he suggested. She had always felt a fondness for the nickname he called her when she was first hatched. Plus, she just thought it was funny because she had a strange sense of ironic humor. *Really strange for a dragon,* he thought. He chuckled, spotting a bird that landed on her shoulder. She didn't even swipe it off. No doubt too worn out from flying to care, and she probably didn't feel the bird anymore than a horse would feel a flea that landed on its rump. He asked her once why they didn't kill and eat birds and his dragon responded that in addition to birds having no real meat on them, dragons felt connected to all animals of the sky in some way. Hopel just thought that was strange, because for as much pride as dragons had, he couldn't imagine them relating to something that seemed as insignificant as a bird just because it had wings. *In comparison to a mighty dragon— well, there was no comparison*, he let the thought fade away. Yet, when he and Little One were resting, it appeared that Little One actually enjoyed watching the small birds fly and look for worms. He remembered a conversation that they had a while back.

If the dragons respect the birds, why is it then that we are required to kill a mermabird to bond with you? Hopel asked his dragon in mind-speak one day when they were revisiting this concept that all dragons felt connected to birds.

No dragon requires you to kill the mermabird. That is a human custom for your village to decide who is worthy to bond. Why is it that you can't get feathers without killing the bird?

You would have to be there to understand. It isn't the easiest thing in the world to get those feathers.

Well, I'm not sure that they are real birds anyway. I think they are some kind of magical fish that turns into some kind of magical bird. What kind of magic this is… I don't know. I'm only a young dragon after all. I do know that we don't require you to kill it to bond. However, we don't interfere with your will to do it either.

Well, where did the custom come from then? Hopel asked his dragon.

I'm not sure. Some human person got it in his or her head that you needed to be worthy to bond with us and came up with this challenge to decide if you are. It isn't like you humans don't have contests for everything, right?

Well, yes we do, but I think it is sad if we are killing the beautiful mermabird for nothing then. Why is it that you dragons never spoke up about this before?

Perhaps we have. I'm telling you right now, aren't I? Why do you think the other bonded have not done the same? You humans aren't anxious to change your customs.

Indeed she was right on both accounts, Hopel thought. Then changing the subject, he continued to mind-speak to her. *Well why did you choose me then?*

Don't you think other humans have climbed those cliffs before I chose you? We either stay hidden when we don't want to bond, or if someone isn't meant for us, but still tries to take us, our parents chase him or her away. The feather didn't decide for me to choose you. The Maker assigned me to you and choosing you was something that I felt called to do. In counterpart, you had felt called to me as well, and this is how we found each other and bonded.

Touched by the Creator to be my protector, yes? Hopel asked.

Yes. Little One said simply. *As were you touched by the Maker to be my bonded and in some ways my protector as well, at least when I was in my egg.*

He liked how intimately she expressed herself when speaking about the Creator. He liked her use of the term "Maker" and he wondered if dragons had been designed for this purpose… a purpose that included protecting and guiding humans towards the ultimate goals given by the Creator… goals to love and sacrifice… for he loved her, and he would sacrifice everything for her, even if the sacrifice included cleaning her big, sharp teeth of gross stuck meat… a chore no Lexonite bonded liked.

Anyway, shaking himself out of his reverie of this past conversation, Hopel noticed that this particular bird seemed to be resting on her. Hopel, looking closely, noticed the bird seemed a bit odd. The colors were unusual— nothing that Hopel had ever seen in an animal before. The bird looked like it wore a covering of varying layers of gold and silver feathers. The thing that amazed him the most though was that the tip of the bird's beak looked like it was dipped in gold. In fact, he could have sworn that it was the same bird he noticed at their last resting stop because he couldn't imagine there was more than one bird that looked so remarkable. The strangest thing about the bird was that it actually seemed to have an intoxicating fragrance radiating from it. Never before had any animal smelled so heavenly. It was almost as if a delectable lavender scent was emitted off it and relaxed those around it. Perhaps, he thought, this was nature's way of protecting the bird.

Little One was starting to wake. *I see you are already awake.* She mumbled sleepily to him in mind-speak.

"Yeah, I woke up a while ago, but I wanted you to rest as long as you needed because I know how tired you must be from flying."

Do you now... when was the last time you flew? She chortled in that somewhat irritating dragon way she had of laughing.

"You know what I mean," he quickly retorted, glaring at her. "Besides hanging on and staying seated on a dragon saddle isn't exactly that easy either, even with a lap strap."

Hmmm, you seem a little grumpy... maybe you should have slept longer yourself.

"I'm not grumpy, but sometimes you tease incessantly, and I'm just growing anxious. The council sent us to check out the rumors of strange occurrences in the north, and we have yet to see anything. I'm starting to miss home. I'd like to know if Nohm and Lisbeth got a feather and made it through the Primitus Challenge as one of the first five. Plus, I don't know if we are even going in the right direction."

Anxious to get home to see Lisbeth? Little One teased him again, not even fazed by his reprimand.

Hopel refused to acknowledge her ribbing this time as he replied, "The point is that I think we are going in the wrong direction and getting nowhere."

No, we are going in the right direction.

"How do you even know?" he asked.

A little bird told me.

"Huh? Usually for humans that expression figuratively means a person told you and you don't want to tell me who that person is, but there is no one here but us, so how could you know?" Hopel was utterly confused.

Well, I mean it ***literally****.* Little One pointed her head in the direction of the bird resting on her.

"Yeah, right! Hopel figured Little One was messing with him again. Well, if you want to act all mysterious and pretend you know where we are going, go ahead, but I'm not buying it." To not believe one's dragon is almost unheard of because their bond ran so deep that usually they could detect any dishonesty between them and there would be no reason for dishonesty anyway between the bonded, but Little One, whether because of youth or personality, liked to jape and pull pranks so much that Hopel was careful with what she did and said. He knew that despite their bond she could pull off deceiving him without him knowing it, if only because her motives were still pure… she thought she was bringing him laughter. The problem is that he often didn't find her tricks humorous.

Believe me or don't. Little One shrugged her dragon shoulders. *We still need to get flying and right now I'm the only one with any ideas, sooo…*

"So fine. Let's go," Hopel agreed as he put the saddle on her.

As they were flying, Hopel was checking behind him and could have sworn the little bird was following them. *No,* he thought. *I must be imagining it because she put the ridiculous thought in my head that the bird could talk to her.*

4

Why were Sanchezo and his dragon, Cordo, in this cave? Candade had started to explore caverns searching for Swish when she saw them. Sanchezo appeared even less human and Cordo even less dragon than usual. Cordo's gray dragon skin sagged on his body while his mouth was dripping with rancid saliva. His master's, Sanchezo's, skin appeared equally gray as well, or at least what she could see of it appeared gray since he was wearing a black robe, which covered most of his body. What she could see clearly were Sanchezo's eyes. They glowed red! She could hardly believe what she was seeing. Sanchezo was staring at something on the ground while mumbling something inaudible, and his eyes glowed red as he spoke!

An eerie fog engulfed both him and his dragon with black smoke swirling between and around them. Candade tried her hardest to hear him and to see what he was looking at, but she couldn't quite see it with the swirling fog surrounding him, blocking him and whatever it was he was looking at from her view. She couldn't hear him either. She tried to sneak closer, but paused when she saw Cordo sniffing the air. Frozen in place, she barely breathed.

Unable to move, she was able to see the reason for Cordo's extra salivating. The dragon was distracted with snapping at and pursuing a bat, which was flying deeper within the cave.

Finally, she inched forward, which allowed her to see what Sanchezo was staring at. She was surprised when it appeared to just be a stone, but she was even more surprised when the stone seemed to shake and emit a blood red, glowing light. The stone was lying on top of what looked like an oddly triangularly shaped, pure black stalagmite with red streaks from the stone's emitted light swirling within it. *Is the red vibrating stone reflecting light onto the stalagmite making it look like it had fiery, blood red streaks in it too? Is that why Sanchezo's eyes are reflected red? Why would a stone vibrate?* She had to find out.

Sneaking in even closer to get a better look, she thought she saw a current of the fiery red waves flowing within the stone; and glowing deeply, it shined and vibrated with a ghostly, dark red light that really was penetrating throughout the stalagmite as if it couldn't be contained in the stone itself. Her concentration on the red light, she hadn't realized that she had stepped onto an area of loose stones. With a gasp, she stumbled over a rock, and then quickly put her hand over her mouth, fearful that he had heard her.

She knew he had when Sanchezo abruptly stopped his mumbling and turned towards her. Heartbeat quickening, she held her breath and inched backwards. Then he laughed in that crazy, maniacal way that he had, and looked straight at her.

Although she could barely see any other part of him with his dark attire, she could now clearly see his piercing, strange, red glowing eyes. Walking a few steps in her direction, he pointed straight at her as she tried to inch further back where she hoped he couldn't see her. Instead of moving back, however, she lost control of her own body and feet. She felt pulled by some unknown force towards him and then remembered how he had used magic before to ensnare Hopel and his dragon before the council rescued them. If he could do that with a dragon, what chance did she have, and no one even knew she was here?

Inch by inch she fought against the pull but could do nothing. Continuing to eerily laugh, he spoke her name as she was forced forward. He ominously whispered, looking straight at her, "You return, my dearest. No need to be afraid of little old me… come closer."

"What do you want with me? Leave us alone," Candade felt herself calling out into the darkness.

"But I have plans for you, my dear." he responded, approaching her slowly.

Just as he was closing in on her, about to grab her, she felt a pair of ice-white wings wrap around her in a protective barrier. It happened quickly and startled her. Then, a strong and comforting whisper floated towards her… *wake up*. Startled out of her trance, she woke up then and found herself at home in her own bed. She sat straight up in a cold sweat, fear infiltrating every fiber of her being… a nightmare… that's all it was, she told herself. Her whole body was shaking while she still tried to reconcile herself to her surroundings and figure out where she was.

Trying to clear her head of the fog that persisted in clouding her mind, she was still having trouble accepting that she was home in bed. She looked around again to convince herself that she was indeed safe. Slowly, heart beating fast and still shaking, she began to finally accept that it had only been a nightmare. Ever since he had kidnapped her, she'd had these bad dreams. What was Sanchezo still doing in her dreams, and why couldn't she feel her dragon?

"Swish, Swish, can you hear me? Where are you? Was that a dream? Was it you in my dream helping me? Please answer." Candade whispered the words aloud as well as calling out to him in her mind, even though deep down she knew those white wings didn't belong to her green and brown-camouflaged dragon. Indeed, all she heard and felt in return was silence… there was no response from her dragon, and it was just a bad dream.

When Candade woke the next morning, she sat up abruptly, and immediately put her hands to her head. Her head throbbed painfully, and she felt empty deep inside of her. Again, she wondered where her dragon was. Her nightmares hadn't ended with the one about Sanchezo and the cave either. She had another one with Taylor, the man she had killed to protect her dragon and her friends when he was trying to control her dragon and kill her friends. Or at least, she thought that is why she had killed him. She was unable to forget his shocked look or his eyes as they glazed over when she had put her sword through him and said, "For Nater". Nater was her brother and he was murdered by Taylor to steal his bonded dragon egg. Why did she say that? Surely, she didn't kill Taylor for revenge. A dragon rider fought for justice, not for revenge, right? Is this why Taylor continued to haunt her? Either way, if she hadn't killed him, he would have killed them. Her friends had assured her that she had no choice. Her dragon, Swish, also had no choice when he killed Taylor's dragon… well, it was never Taylor's dragon. It was her brother's dragon before Taylor killed her brother, and it only hatched after Sanchezo manipulated it with dark magic, and whatever creature it was that hatched was no longer a real dragon anyway, so Swish was just putting it out of its misery. Both had acted in self-defense and these doubts that invaded her thoughts now were coming from no good place.

She put her hands over her eyes as if to block out the nightmarish memories. It didn't work, and with Nohm and

Swish gone, there was no one that she could talk to about the nightmares. She was all alone. *I should see Breker the herbalist today and try to get him to give me more herbs to help me to sleep tonight*, she thought. *Maybe he could give me something that would prevent nightmares and headaches too.* She didn't want to go through another night like the last one, and while the herbs that she was taking did help her to sleep she wasn't sure what good it was doing her if she was regularly awakened by nightmares.

5

Hopel was crouching close to Little One to try and stay warm as they flew through the northern mountains. The heat that she emitted bubbled around him in a barrier that protected him from the cold. Below the clouds, the glitter of snow-peaked mountains looked lovely and inviting, though he knew the opposite to be true. These mountains were filled with danger. He was starting to notice that the appearance of living plants and animals was scarce. Usually, there were certain animals and plants that still thrived in these northern mountains, but he didn't see anything living anywhere, and this wasn't normal. *I wonder if this was what the council was hearing about and worried about, but what would be causing this?*

Little One, he communicated with mind-speak rather than shouting over the wind. *Do you think we should land?*

For what purpose? She replied. *We still don't know what to look for.*

To rest for one thing, he told her. *Plus, I want to look around on the ground, and we also need to eat.*

Except that there is nothing alive down there for me to eat. You forget with my dragon vision that I can see for miles in every direction.

Do you have any idea why nothing is alive down there?

No, I don't see a reason for it anywhere, but there is something else… a feeling or a sense that I am getting of despondency or forlornness… I guess you humans would call it 'despair'. It doesn't matter. Humans might choose to stop thriving, but plants and animals do not have the choice to stop thriving. Something is destroying everything. There should be life.

What do you mean, 'humans might choose to stop thriving…"

I mean that grown humans who are beaten down have the will to thrive again if they so choose. A plant or an animal doesn't have that will. Animals and plants thrive if their environment permits it.

You are wise for such a young dragon.

We dragons inherit wisdom.

However, you are not modest. Hopel laughed. Quickly getting serious again though, he agreed with Little One, *Something is definitely wrong. Let's land here; so we can explore a little more from below.*

Okay, but remember we are on an exploratory mission to report back on what we see from a distance only. We have no back up out here. I will not put your life in danger. So, we will only land and rest for a few minutes.

Seems like she is being a little cowardly for a dragon, Hopel thought, although he was careful to guard his mind from his dragon. He wouldn't want her to know he was thinking that. An offended dragon was not a fun dragon even to its bonded, and he was sure *she* would think *he* was just being overly *rash* because sometimes he got it into his head that she could handle anything.

They landed at the base of one of the mountains, near a large lake. Hopel looked around for signs of animal tracks in the thin layer of snow that covered the ground but saw nothing. He didn't know why he even looked since Little One had just said there was no life for miles. Still, he had hoped she was wrong. The shrill wind blasted and bit through his clothes. He shivered and moved closer to Little

One for the warmth that radiated from her body. For as far as he could see, snow-covered land abounded in every direction, and with the exception of the towering trees, which swayed violently in the raging wind, it was just as she had indicated… not even insects were moving. His stomach growled again, and it gave him an idea… even though everything around them seemed dead, Little One could melt some ice, and they could fish for supper. He figured the fish would still be alive as they moved deeper towards the bottom of the lake to avoid the freezing temperatures at the top. Perhaps living in the deeper parts of the lake would enable the fish to avoid whatever was killing the life in this area. His stomach was growling like crazy, and he knew Little One had to be hungry. He was thankful for mind-speak because he didn't have to try to yell over the wind.

After relaying his thoughts to her, she answered him, ***You** mean **I** fish for our supper, right? Not 'we', and you forget that though I am capable of warming my body and surviving the cold depths for a very limited amount of time, I don't want to do it! Almost no dragon does. We despise icy water, and the lakes in these northern mountains are not like the ones back home, if we are exposed long enough, it will kill us.*

Her use of the word "almost" stumped Hopel for a minute and almost made him forget his hunger, but rather than ask what she meant, he comforted his dragon and responded with the affection that he felt. *Well, I didn't mean for you to stay under there long, but if you don't want to do it, fine. I don't want to put you at risk either.* He figured it was his stomach doing the thinking now anyway. *This is getting us nowhere. I think we should just go back and report what we have seen. We have no idea why, but things are dying here. I mean there is nothing, not even a northern white hare anywhere, right? Northern hares, at least, should have survived here by digging in the snow and eating the mosses and lichens.*

Little One shook her head no. *It is just as I told you from the air. There is nothing alive down here. The sooner we get back, the sooner we can eat real food since you are almost completely out of what you brought in the saddle, and I haven't been able to hunt in a long time… hunger is another thing a dragon won't survive, and apparently a human can't think hungry.* She chuckled then, and Hopel, used to his dragon's ribbing, ignored her.

As they were debating and conversing a large shadow flew overhead, startling them. Surprised because nothing seemed alive for miles, Hopel jumped up and immediately climbed into his saddle on Little One. Without missing a beat, he yelled, "Little One fly up there and see who or what it is." He thought the shadow had to be a dragon as it was gigantic.

Little One took off with a typical dragon roar. Flying higher and higher, she was unable to catch up to the dragon, but followed it as fast as she could.

Is that… It looks like… Hopel floundered for the words. How could it be?

Yes, it looks like Swish, but if it is, he isn't responding to my mind-speak and his rider certainly is not with him. Whoever it is seems distant and like a stranger to me. When I try to mind-speak with him, I feel… foggy.

Foggy?

It is the only way that I know how to describe what it is that I am sensing.

Okay, follow him, but be careful. This is odd. Hopel knew that all dragons could mind-speak to each other. Even wild dragons could communicate with other dragons. In fact, it was a choice that the wild dragons made to allow an egg to choose to bond with a Lexonite and mind-speak with their bonded in order to facilitate the relationship between humans and dragons… a legacy that was established ages and ages ago for the betterment of both races… but while they only spoke to their human bond, they could choose to speak to any of their own kind, and usually they understood each other as clearly as two human beings would understand each other if the two humans were talking to each other in the same language.

It looks like he is headed for that cave, Little One told him.

If it is Swish, why would he be way out here without Candade? Hopel was perplexed.

I don't know, but he just landed, and he is headed inside.

Okay, we'll land too, but try to stay hidden in the shadows. Fortunately, Hopel knew Little One's dark colors made it very hard to see her in the shadows and nearly impossible at night. Thus, it would also be virtually impossible to see her in a cave, and since dragon riders' attire tended to match their dragons, the color of Hopel's quiver and chain mail armor was also black, which made him hard to see in the dark too.

As they crept into the dark cave, Hopel thought he recognized a disturbing voice. He hoped against hope that he was wrong.

Is that voice Sanchezo's? It can't be. Even in mind-speak, Hopel's stunned thoughts were barely a whisper; fear almost prevented him from asking her the question.

It would appear so, Little One answered, the regret and fear obvious in her voice though she communicated in mind-speak as well. Her body quivered. It was not that long ago that Sanchezo was able to control her with dark magic, and she had lost all her ability to move and fly on her own. A dragon doesn't usually have to fear anything, much less being overpowered, so she wasn't likely to forget that feeling of helplessness any time soon.

They could hear Sanchezo's words, but could barely make them out. It sounded like he was speaking to Swish and welcoming him back and telling him what a good dragon he was for having come. It sounded like someone else was there too and was speaking to Sanchezo, but he didn't see whoever it was because a black fog that he couldn't see through surrounded the voice. Even though he couldn't make the strange voice out, it felt evil and sinister. The eerie voice was slowly drifting away along with the fog, but even with just Sanchezo there, the darkness and despair he felt in the cave was suffocating.

Did he just hear Sanchezo tell Swish that Candade would follow him here? But how could she without riding Swish? That made no sense even for the crazy Sanchezo. None of this made sense. Swish wouldn't come here himself.

Little One, do you think Sanchezo captured her again? He got no response from his dragon who was now staring at something that glowed in the cave. Was that a glowing stone that he was seeing? *Little One! Listen to me!* He still got no reply from her, so he shouted her name now in mind-speak while taking her head in both his hands and making her look at him. Thankfully, because they were crouched as close to the cave bottom as possible, he was able to reach it. *Snap out of it. Look at me. Is Candade here?*

She shook her head rapidly, shaking off his hands along with whatever was distracting her before she responded. *Ugh, I feel... weird... I can't focus, but I don't think so, I get no sense or smell of her. We need to leave and report this while we can. Plus, I need to keep us safe.* Little One backed out slowly, anxious to get away from Sanchezo and that glowing light. Plus, she knew that if Sanchezo was here that meant his dragon Cordo was here somewhere too. She was still a young dragon and Sanchezo had already proved that Hopel and Little One were no match for them.

Hopel agreed with her. They needed to get out of there. Something was still glowing in the center of the cave, and Hopel still felt like he needed to scream at her in mind-speak to communicate. Whatever Sanchezo was doing with the object was still trying to draw and distract his dragon, and it attracted her attention in such a strange way that he was afraid she would forget where she was and walk right out to Sanchezo.

He could see that the light already appeared to have Swish mesmerized. He was staring directly at it, and he wasn't moving away. Surrounding Swish were creatures that Hopel had never seen before. One of them looked like a warped version of the northern white hare. Only it's head was twice the normal size of a northern white hare, and it had fangs coming out of its head.

What did he do to those animals? He asked Little One in mind-speak. *Is that why there are no animals left in the mountains?* She could only shake her head in reply.

Swish stepped onto one of the warped creatures as he drew nearer the stone, completely unaware of anything beside the light that was drawing him. The other creatures squealed and growled as they quickly scampered out of his way. Hopel hoped the distraction would allow them to escape.

He gestured wildly at Little One… *Back up now while we have time,* but she appeared confused again, so he also pushed against her, which would mean little to nothing to her unless she snapped out of it. Finally, with the combination of pushing, gesturing wildly, and mind-speak, she started unsteadily backwards until she stumbled over a boulder, which caused a plethora of rocks to come tumbling off the ledge making a clattering noise.

"What was that?" Sanchezo snapped and then screamed out loud. "Cordo, where are you? That dragon is never where I need him to be." He appeared to be speaking to Swish, but the dragon did not turn to look at him, much less answer. He was still staring at the red glow. "I guess I'll have to go and look for myself."

Just as he was beginning his approach down the tunnel where they hid, Cordo came bounding down a different tunnel, apparently chasing a bat, which was flapping its wings wildly in its attempt to escape. "Cordo, knock it off." Sanchezo screamed. "You are going to bring this whole cave down on us. No wonder rocks are falling down everywhere!"

Little One and Hopel could hear Sanchezo screaming as Cordo roared at the bat, and it was the distraction they needed. They retreated faster this time towards the exit, barely escaping before the noise died down.

Let's get out of here, Hopel screamed in mind-speak to his dragon. *Thank goodness, for once, for that awful dragon!*

I second that, she replied as she leapt into the sky. *If only Swish weren't in there. Maybe we could have caused an avalanche to cover the exit and trap Sanchezo.*

Well, that isn't an option because he is in there, Hopel replied as they headed back to the southern lands and their Lexonite village where they needed to go and report to the council.

Hopel, filled with fear that they had been spotted and followed, couldn't help but continue to keep turning around and glance at the cavern, but after a while, he finally breathed a sigh of relief. He was pretty sure that they had escaped since he saw no signs of any other dragon.

Hopel and Little One had been flying for a while without any more mind-speak exchanges, each deep in thought, when Hopel finally spoke to his dragon. *Maybe we shouldn't tell the council until we talk to Candade. If it were you who went into that cave, I would want that courtesy. Maybe Swish has a reason to be there… like we did? Maybe he is on assignment?*

What possible reason could any dragon have for going where Sanchezo was hiding and then staying there and not reporting it? I could tell he wasn't himself because I couldn't even mind-speak to him. I wasn't even myself while we were in there. Plus, If he were on a mission like us, he would have had his rider, Little One replied. *Having you with me is what kept me sane because whatever is in there was trying its hardest to control me. Anyway, the council sent us. So, I think we should report to the council. It is our duty.*

Isn't our duty also to our friends? We will still report to the council, but we will just talk to Candy first. He used Candade's nickname in a further attempt to persuade his dragon to agree with him. Little One had a fondness for Hopel's friends that ran as deep as Hopel's own.

Little One sighed. *As you wish, but if the council finds out that we didn't report to them first, you are going to end up with privy digging duty, and I'm not going to hang around to watch.*

Oh yeah… what if they make you, Hopel retorted.

I'd like to see them try, she replied.

Well, maybe not the humans, but I know a very big dragon on the council that could make you… Hopel quit when she turned around and glared at him with a low growl. He figured then that he was pushing the jab a little too far, and he'd better quit while he was ahead… of sorts. His dragon was not only a prankster, but also she was competitive, and she didn't like to be bested even with verbal cracks by anyone, including her bonded, when she wasn't in the mood. She definitely wasn't in the mood after a close call like they'd just had.

6

Candade felt uneasy gazing at the herbalists' adobe. The sunstar-dried clay home seemed overly dark with vines growing everywhere on it. She figured that made sense since the vines could themselves be a source for some of the herbs they used, but it was still a little creepy. She was unsure where they got all of their herbs because the inside of the house seemed too tightly packed with shelves upon shelves that were filled with an overabundance of dusty, smelly bottles stuffed with substances she'd never heard of and didn't recognize.

Upon entering through the door, she was greeted by Benjess, the herbalist's son. It didn't surprise her that he was there instead of his father. In fact, she didn't remember seeing the herbalist, Breker, for a while now. She knew that Breker would disappear for weeks sometimes, leaving his son in charge now that Benjess' mother had passed. She always had assumed he was out hunting for more herbs, but this time it seemed like he had been gone even longer than usual.

Benjess had been the one helping her the last few months now. She wanted to ask him where his father was, but she felt that would be rude, especially since she knew that Benjess was a very private person. Benjess was dark skinned, like most Lexonites with closely cropped black hair. He was approximately her age, and when they were younger, she had found him averagely attractive. They had been friendly with each other, but she never found him an easy person to get close to since he seemed really shy. Now, since he worked with his father he had to communicate more with people, but he still kept conversations brief and to the point, his face mostly unreadable. "Hi Candade. How can I help you?" He asked her politely now with a slight smile.

"I haven't been sleeping well, and while the herbs that you gave me last time have been helping me to sleep, I wake up with headaches, and I continue to have nightmares which seem as if they are worsening," she answered him hesitantly.

"Have you seen the healers about this?" Benjess inquired.

"No, I don't really want to involve them. It isn't really serious, and I don't want them thinking Swish and I aren't ready for duty again, and I especially don't want to risk the healers telling the council that we shouldn't be assigned anything real," Candade admitted.

"Well, I agree with you about the council," Benjess told her as he prepared her herbs. "I'll just give you a little something more to help you sleep, and you don't have to worry about me telling them anything. We are a hundred percent close mouthed in our store."

It seemed to Candade as if he was taking longer than usual to prepare the herbs and actually conversing with her more than usual too. She didn't need his assurances about being confidential… why would she expect anything less? *What else would a herbalist be?* However, she did feel good that he was siding with her. Since her brother's passing, it had been a while since she felt supported. She wondered if he now appreciated talking with her and was purposely taking longer. There was a time when she thought that he had a crush on her.

Benjess, compatibly, continued on, "I mean… I don't blame you for not wanting them looking over your shoulder for everything. I'm sure you will get back to sleeping normally soon anyway. Anyone who went through what you went through would have some trouble dealing with it afterwards."

"Well, that isn't what I mean either. I'm not having trouble dealing with it. I'm fine," Candade denied. "Maybe I'm just worried about Swish," She didn't even realize that she had said the latter aloud.

"Swish? What is wrong with Swish?" he asked a little too quickly.

Surprised by his immediate interest she paused, unsure as to whether to admit anything to him, especially since this conversation seemed completely out of character for him, but then she finally muttered, "He flew off without telling me anything, and he has been gone longer than ever before, and he never does that…" Her voice dwindled off. She was no longer talking to Benjess but just thinking out loud. "He probably just went hunting and is too far away for us to mind-speak… still, why did I think I heard him whispering to me last night?"

"You did?" Benjess replied with apparent concern.

Candade, now worried that she had shared too much, refrained from saying anything further. Perhaps she worried over nothing, but she was no longer comfortable sharing. She just shrugged her shoulders as an answer.

After an awkward pause, Benjess, realizing that she wasn't going to say anything else, added, "I'm sure he is just hunting and will return soon. I'm increasing your dosage though to help you sleep and hopefully worry less."

After thanking Benjess again for his advice and herbs, Candade started her walk home. *Maybe if Hopel returns soon, Little One could look for Swish, and I wouldn't have to involve anyone else,* she mused. *Then again, could she really trust Hopel?* Sanchezo had hinted that someone related to him had been bonded recently, and while Sanchezo didn't say who it was, only five people had bonded last year and one of them, her brother, had died because of him. If it was true and not just him messing with her mind, whoever this relation is must be distantly related because Sanchezo must be centuries old and only alive due to his magic and dragon bond. Even if Sanchezo forced his dragon, Cordo, to bond to him with dark magic, the dragon's magic would still keep him alive longer. W*hat if it was true though, and it was Hopel who was distantly related to him?* Well, that didn't mean that Hopel would join forces with Sanchezo anyway, and what choice did she have? Swish had never been gone from her for this long. She needed to get someone's help, and she was just being paranoid again worrying about Hopel. Plus, if Swish didn't return soon, the council would know soon enough that something was amiss. She and Swish were one of the bonded pairs who were supposed to fly drills at the celebration ceremony after the five who were chosen to climb the dragon cliffs returned. *Plus, what if something happened to him and that is why he didn't answer her.* No, she shook that thought out of her mind. For sure, she felt she would know if something happened to him even if he wasn't answering her right now.

Candade only made it a short distance before she was startled out of her reverie when she heard her name being called. Lea caught up to her quickly. "Your mom sent me to find you. Apparently, Greecher is looking for you, and you are supposed to report to him," Lea, leaning over and holding her side, was totally out of breath having run the whole time in search of her.

"Ugh. I knew it was going to happen," Candade groaned.

"You knew what was going to happen? Did Swish come back yet?" Lea asked, running her two completely different questions together in her eagerness to know what was going on.

"I knew he was going to single us out for extra work or some kind of punishment because we didn't do well in the practice for the ceremony, and to answer your second question… not yet," Candade replied, the worry obvious in her eyes though she tried to hide it from Lea. "I'm sure he is just off hunting." It wasn't really a fib because he could be off hunting, she thought, and she didn't want Lea to worry or tell anyone else about Swish's odd behavior.

"Hmmm… doesn't sound right, but I don't have a dragon, so I guess I wouldn't know," Lea said tentatively.

"That's right, you don't and you wouldn't," Candade blurted out impatiently before she caught herself and softened her tone. "Anyway Squirt, can you do me a favor? Take my medicine back to my house for me, so I can go find Greecher, please." Candade asked with an apologetic shake of the head and sigh.

"Medicine? Lea took the herbs but held it at a distance from her. Why do you need this stinky medicine? You don't look sick." Lea wrinkled her nose as she feigned distaste, still upset that Candade had sounded rude to her. "Where did you get it?"

"Stinky?"

"Yeah, stinky… you don't smell it?"

"Uh, I smell something, but I don't think the medicine smells, and I'm not sick… it is just… it helps me sleep better. If you must know, I got it from the herbalist," she answered, confused now, her words stumbling over each other. She had a brief passing thought that perhaps it was this odor that she had noticed all along.

"Really, you didn't go to the healers? I doubt the council or Greecher would like that one of their dragon riders went to the herbalist instead of the healers," Lea admonished her.

"Really Lea, the medicine is nothing, and I don't want to involve them, so you need to stay out of it." She realized she had started to sound abrupt again due to her growing impatience with Leah or her pounding headache, she didn't know which, and so she softened her tone again. "Plus, I don't have time to talk about it. You know how Greecher gets. Just promise me you won't say anything and would you please just take it back to my room?" Candade pressed.

"Well, okay. I guess," Lea reluctantly agreed.

"Great, Squirt. Thanks. I'll see you later," Candade put the herbs in Lea's hands. In turn, Lea took the bag and held it away from her while pinching her nose. Candade just shook her head and shoved the young girl towards her home. She felt a little guilty for being short with Lea, but she didn't have time to worry about that now and was just relieved that the girl still listened. She figured she could make it up to Lea later.

She could only imagine what was in store for her when she found Greecher. Not only was she going to end up doing "penance" for the drills, but also because she was by herself, she had to avoid him finding out that Swish was missing.

7

On the way back to their canoes, Nohmran and Elizabeth were chatting about the best way to travel back to the village when Courtnia interrupted them, glaring angrily, "You two talk a lot. Haven't you ever heard of staying quiet to keep unwanted predators away… especially in this forest. I know I had no problem finding you because you were so noisy."

"Hmmm… I can see why you prefer to do things alone… anti-social a little are we? I guess we have been okay so far since we are still living," Lisbeth retorted sarcastically. "Maybe our chatting is scaring the animals away… did you ever think of…"

Just as she was about to finish her sentence, a raucous shriek, which was definitely not from any animal they had ever heard before, trumpeted loudly. The cacophony was in perfect timing to affirm Courtnia's opinion about how they should be walking. It sent chills down Lisbeth's arms. Considering the forest's noises and how Nohmran agreed with her feeling that they were being followed, Lisbeth couldn't hide the anxiety from her face even if she tried.

"Yeah, right.. I wouldn't bet on that," Courtnia whispered, and all three young people grew quiet.

Peering up into the thick canopy of branches overhead, Nohmran noticed the animal that he thought had made the sound. Pointing up at it, he said, "There, I think that bird in that branch made the screeching sound. It doesn't look too scary."

Both girls looked up to see a bird that resembled a hawk peering down at them. Strangely enough its eyes almost looked intelligent, as if it was weighing them as a potential food source.

Luckily, it must have decided that they were too big to eat because it didn't move off of its branch.

"I guess it wouldn't hurt to send a prayer up to the High God," Lisbeth added with a shiver.

"High God? I don't know if it would hurt, but I doubt it would help either," Courtnia snorted. "And High God? What, do you have other, lower gods?"

"No, it is just a sign of respect," Nohmran answered.

"Well, we call him the Creator or the Maker, and no matter what you call him, I doubt he is helping us," Courtnia snapped. "I know my life wasn't easy and no one helped me."

"Whoa, slow down with the attitude," Nohm answered. "Even if you don't believe he is helping us, there is no reason for you to stomp on our faith and besides how do you know he isn't helping you? We don't expect life to be easy. It is never easy, but if you stay positive and believe all hardships have meaning and the Creator still loves us, you grow stronger. Things could be much worse, you know. Plus, if you don't ask, you're not even giving him a chance to help you and ease the hardship."

"Why would I have to ask? If he were the Maker of everything, he would know I need help, right? As far as a reason, how about the reason is that I have learned to rely on myself and not just hope, like some weakling, that someone comes down from the sky to save me, and I don't need anyone telling me otherwise," Courtnia retorted and stomped off ahead of them.

"Well, okay then," Lisbeth, shaking her head, looked at her cousin and shrugged her shoulders while sending up a prayer for safety, good judgment, and strength. Then, at the last minute, she added one for Courtnia albeit a little reluctantly. "I don't think it would do any good to tell her that it is written in our holy book to ask for help when we need it and not just expect him to know we need help even if he absolutely does already know it."

"I like when people ask me for help and not just expect it or assume it, so it makes sense to me. I think the Creator loves us and wants to have a relationship with us too and you can't have relationships without communication, and I don't think as parents we protect our children all the time. Sometimes it is about making our children stronger. Otherwise, we wouldn't be trying to become dragon riders. But you are right… I don't think she would be interested in our holy book right now," Nohmran agreed.

They were almost back to the boat when she was glad that she had sent up that prayer asking for help.

The forest had finally changed into a less ominous looking forest when she started getting a strange feeling again that something was off. At first, everything seemed as the Creator intended. The tree branches shivered slightly from the cool breeze, and their multicolored leaves floated peacefully in the air or littered the ground, painting it in various hues that looked like a supreme artist had taken his brush to the world, in order to show what warmth and comfort in nature should look like. Yet, looking more intently through those less ominous branches, Lisbeth thought she noticed a dark area completely depleted of the beauty around it where there were no trees and no branches, a deep dark empty space where no artist was permitted to paint. In this little piece of the forest, though beauty surrounded it, was a dark void of nothingness.

"Nohm, look at the dark space over there. Could that be a cave? It is as black as night though everything around it is the opposite." Usually the Whispering Forest was noisy with sounds from the abundant animals that lived in it, but for some reason there were no sounds where they walked, which was also odd because this part of the forest seemed so peaceful and beautiful. Getting a little closer and peering deep into the empty space, she thought she saw two narrow glows of light.

"It's too quiet," she whispered to him, wrinkling her nose. "And something doesn't feel right… or smell right for that matter." For some reason, the forest grew silent and a vicious scent that smelled of two-day-old dead fish and excrement thickened as they walked nearer the cave towards where they left their boat.

"Yeah, it is odd," he agreed, but before he could say anything else about it, a massive cat-like creature slithered out of the dark space and jumped in front of them. Its huge black body stood as high as their shoulders. The creature was tall. Its head was as large as any dragon head that they had ever seen, but uglier and with fangs protruding from its jaws… fangs that dripped and reeked of rotted fish-like smelling saliva. Its long reptile-like tail had spikes extending from it and the smell… it's body reeked also… a smell worse than excrement, he decided. The glow or light that Lisbeth thought she saw must have been its eyes, which were large, horizontal, elongated eyes that did not blink… *like a snake's*, he thought. "It's the Crotaw," he whispered, "It's not supposed to be above the ground. It shouldn't be here! Whatever you do, move slowly. The jaws and the tail are deadly."

"Well someone should tell the Crotaw that it isn't

supposed to be here and for that matter tell it that its smell is deadly," Courtnia replied sarcastically, gagging, while backing up as slowly as she could and hoping it wouldn't notice.

"Uh," I think it is all deadly… look at the claws," Lisbeth whispered. She raised her arm slowly to pull out an arrow, but stopped mid-motion when the movement seemed to make the creature pounce forward a few feet.

"Don't move or do anything to startle it," Nohmran kept whispering.

"Well, what should we do… pray?" Even then Courtnia managed to still grumble out the comment sarcastically.

"Creator, Maker, High God… please protect us," Lisbeth responded with complete sincerity in answer to Courtnia's sarcasm, never taking her eyes off the Crotaw. Miraculously, as if in response to her prayer, or after a debate with itself about whether it would slaughter them, it seemed as if the creature was going to continue to move on since it sniffed the air and started moving back towards the dark area that she assumed was its cave. Lisbeth hoped it decided that three of them were too many to take on for an easy meal and that the battle wouldn't be worth it. She had no sooner breathed out a sigh of relief than her terror was renewed by an action from Courtnia.

"Again, I said I rely on myself." Unexpectedly, Courtnia, in one quick angry motion, pulled out her dagger whip. This action, which happened in an instant, had the creature whirling around and moving in towards them again.

"Fool, stop antagonizing it," Lisbeth spoke loud enough for her to hear. *Why did she have to do that? It looked like it was leaving.* Stunned by Courtnia's repressed anger-driven foolishness, Lisbeth and Nohmran simultaneously pulled out their quiver and arrows, but then stood completely still and didn't release them in hopes that the Crotaw would back off again. Courtnia, however, was still swinging her dagger whip, which was keeping the creature at a distance, if only temporarily, and no doubt helped it decide that it would not retreat.

Lisbeth decided to try another approach and started to scream at it. "Hey you… yeah you… get out of here! Get out of here! She waved her arrows and arms wildly.

At that moment, they knew there was no hoping that it would retreat. The Crotaw creature mobilized its tail to attack the nearest person and whacked the whip out of Courtnia's hands. With a scream Courtnia looked down at her arm… an abrasion, nothing more, but it immediately began to burn and sting. She would be okay if they could get out of this and she could get to the healers quickly in case it was poisonous.

Immediately after its attack, Nohmran and Lisbeth released their arrows, which for a minute only managed to distract it from pouncing on Courtnia as it spun on its tail to see what had attacked it. Peering at them now, it shook the arrows free but then, as if deciding that it would deal with them later, it half slithered, half whirled back to Courtnia and with an angry growl jumped towards her head, its mouth wide open.

It was just as the Crotaw was about to clench its jaws on her that something jumped out in mid-air and struck the creature on its side, knocking it off balance for a moment.

"It's a dog!" Courtnia screamed, shocked.

No sooner had she said it than the Crotaw was back on its feet and swiping its tail towards the humongous black and gray dog. The dog jumped back just in time, still growling and barking at the creature. The Crotaw swiped at it with its claws and must have made contact because the dog suddenly whined. Still, the dog didn't back down. He kept barking and growling, and moving its body in and out of reach of the Crotaw's claws.

At the same time, because of the distraction, Lisbeth

and Nohmran were able to keep attacking it with arrows, hoping one of the hits would be enough to bring it down.

Courtnia inched her way towards her dagger whip, but the Crotaw saw her and jerked its body in her direction again. Even with all the attacks going on around it, the Crotaw persisted, intent on getting to her.

Within moments of the Crotaw jerking towards Courtnia, the dog moved in on the opposite side and bit the Crotaw's tail. If the Lexonite youths weren't in the midst of trying to save their lives, they might have even thought it comical how the dog weaved in and out, expertly attacking and biting its tail when the Crotaw was turned towards one of them. It wasn't going to kill the Crotaw but it gave them enough time to continue shooting arrows at it. "Nohm", Lisbeth panted with exhausted worry oozing out of her voice, "I'm almost out of arrows and this thing won't die."

"Me too." Nohmran breathed out tiredly. "Die Crotaw already," he said as he shot another arrow directly at its head and between its eyes, but still the arrows did not stop it.

Finally, with the creature distracted by the arrows, Courtnia was able to reach her whip. Swinging it around her head and shoulders to gather momentum, she catapulted the spear head directly into the Crotaw's chest where she assumed its heart should be. It growled one more time and finally fell to the ground.

When it was all over they rushed towards the dog that was now lying down on its side whining. "He's hurt," Courtnia cried. "We have to help it." Blood was seeping out through the dense, abundant fur on the dog's right side.

"We need to get the medicine and bandages from our emergency kit, Nohm. I know it is hopeful, but I think this dog was sent to us from the Creator. He appeared just in time to save us." Lisbeth's voice was still shaking from the close encounter they had just had.

"I don't know why or where it came from, but it

definitely saved me." Courtnia didn't reply with one of her sarcastic comments this time. Instead, she seemed intent on helping the animal.

Nohm returned with the medicine, but when he approached Courtnia to help her, she waved him over to treat the dog first.

"He is so big that I'm not sure how we will move him, much less get him home to the healers for more help, and he is definitely going to need more help. I know the medicine I'm using now on him won't be enough," he said as he applied the medicine. "Wow, he is the biggest dog that I have ever seen."

When he was done working on the dog he'd used most of the medicine that they had brought. Then, he applied the leftover ointment and bandages to Courtnia's arm too. She silently winced at the pain, but still did not speak up. Nohm might not have respected her impulses, but he admired her bravery.

"We'll have to make a stretcher to carry him," Lisbeth stated. "It will slow us down, and we might not make it back before the other challengers to be one of the first five."

"He saved our lives!" Courtnia glared at them. "How could you even suggest that we don't help him?" She hadn't moved from the dog's side and rested the dog's head on her lap, cooing to him that he would be all right.

"We are not suggesting that we leave him to die. We want to help him too, obviously, but we also just wanted you to be aware that if we try to take him back, we will lose time and your dream of being a dragon rider might be over before it even really began. If we are all in agreement that we are going to do this though, we just want you to know what you are risking," she retorted, but even as she was saying it, Nohm moved to make the stretcher.

"Well then, we better hurry," Nohm said, gesturing to Courtnia to get up and help.

"It is good we almost made it back to the boats before this happened. "If the *Creator...*" Lisbeth emphasized the word while looking directly at Courtnia, "sent us this guy to help us, I don't think he would want us abandoning him now either."

Lisbeth looked at the Crotaw in amazement. All their weapons protruding out of its now dead body said more than words could ever say for just how lucky they had been. She didn't know if this animal was as bad as the one that had attacked her friends, Hopel and Cleto, but she didn't imagine it could have been much worse. They just barely made it out of this alive and probably wouldn't have if it weren't for this incredible dog appearing at just the right time. She might not understand all of it, but one thing that she knew for sure... this forest was ominous even when it started to look peaceful. When they were done taking care of the dog and making the stretcher, they would have to retrieve those weapons from the Crotaw and get out of there pronto. She knew that she wasn't looking forward to trying to yank their weapons out of its thick, stinky hide, but she would make quick work of it if she could.

8

U*gh, it is hot,* Candade thought. *I hope Greecher doesn't give me outside work in this heat.* The sunstar was choosing now to stretch its arms out and hug their land tightly in a warm embrace. Sweat was pouring down Candade's face as she walked, and she felt like her skin was frying. The air was still and calm with no breeze to pamper her face and alleviate the heat. She moaned. *Swish would love this weather, but I sure don't.* Everything reminded her of Swish and she agonized over where he was. It was so rare that she didn't know where her bonded partner was that she couldn't fathom what was going on with him. *Swish, if you can hear me, please come home now. Greecher wants us.* She called out to him in mind-speak, but she felt no tingling sensation in her mind, which would precede an answer from Swish. There was only silence.

Looking ahead, she saw Greecher putting the saddle on his dragon, Brisk. Greecher, gruff and old, resembled his dragon a little with that bright silver-gray hair on his head, since Brisk was a beautiful silver color with streaks of black everywhere, well everywhere except on his head… his head was pure silver and striking to look at. It made her want to stare at his head. Actually, she felt compelled to look at both of their heads side by side to see which was a brighter silver, she chuckled to herself briefly at the thought and was glad for the brief departure from her serious thoughts. She thought Brisk sensed her admiration of him because he always seemed to like her. He was looking at her in a curious manner right now, and she wondered if he knew what she was thinking even though they weren't bonded.

"'bout time, young lady. Where is your dragon?" Greecher asked as soon as he saw her.

"Uh… he is out hunting," she answered quietly. She told herself again that she wasn't lying because it could be true.

"Well, call him. I want you both for this," Greecher told her gruffly as he climbed on Brisk. "We are going to do some more drills to make sure you are working in sync with your bond for the ceremony. I don't want any more of that tomfoolery I saw at practice.

"I can't," she avoided meeting his eyes.

"What do you mean you *can't*?" he asked, turning and staring directly at her.

"Uh… he is hunting, but he is out of mind-speak range. I already tried," she met his eyes.

"I expect a little honesty, or you can go do privy duty right now," Greecher's reputation of being a tough trainer was not without truth. He wasn't going to accept anything but the truth, and he laid out the worst job to make sure he got it. So much for his dragon liking her… that wasn't going to get her anywhere. Well, if she just had to forage for plants that wouldn't be bad, but working on any of the privy drainage systems… no thank you.

"Honestly, I don't know where he is. I'm guessing he is probably hunting. He didn't tell me where he was going, and he hasn't answered me since he left." Candade, mumbling again, could barely get out the words.

"Which was when?" Greecher pressed.

" A moon and a half ago," she avoided his look, but didn't bother avoiding the truth now… to herself or to him.

"What… a moon and a half? Have you reported this to the council?"

"No. I… I'm sure he'll be back soon," she stammered.

"Are you?" He turned to Brisk then, and she knew he was mind-speaking between just the two of them. She waited, fidgeting from one foot to the other. Finally he turned back to her. "It seems Brisk can't reach him either. Being unable to speak to your bonded this long shouldn't happen. We need to speak to the council immediately about this."

Candade groaned. In addition to the emptiness, the hole, that was deep within her from Swish's absence, she felt like a failure. Was she the first one to ever lose contact with her bonded? Of course she was. How would it even happen to anyone else? Did Swish stop loving her? Without realizing it, having that thought pop into her head for even the briefest of moments made her fall even further into the desolation that surrounded her lately. So much for the brief interlude from the somber thoughts she had been having lately. She reluctantly followed Greecher to the council circle where she knew Brisk would have used mind-speak already to summon the other council members.

9

Surprisingly, the Lexonite youth were making good time returning from the Whispering Forest, taking turns pulling the dog the short distance back to their boats. It was strange because the stretcher actually ended up being too big for the dog by the time they loaded it. *Actually, it almost seems as if the dog shrank a little after its fight while they were building the stretcher. That can't be possible though*, Nohm thought. *In fact, it kind of looks like Krusteau's, the butcher's, dog. Now that really can't be possible although stories abound around that dog being magical because it was said to have been born on the dragon cliffs near a dragon egg. Maybe that is why I am imagining that it is shrinking and imagining that it is Krusteau's dog. I've heard too many stories about that dog.*

It whimpered as they pulled the stretcher, but otherwise it made no movement. Nohm wondered if they were doing the right thing since it probably wouldn't even live. "It will be alright, Shadow." Courtnia told the dog when it whimpered. She had already named it. "We are almost there now."

"Where is your boat?" Nohm asked her.

"It's by yours." I pulled it in right after you two got there.

"Okay, well that will make it easier. I'll put Shadow in my boat since I am the strongest, and then we can try to stay together when we row our boats back. That way, if I need a break, since Shadow is so heavy, we can switch boats." He offered his plan.

"That sounds fair," Courtnia agreed. "Plus, I am strong too. I wasn't born big boned for nothing.

He smiled. He wasn't about to argue with her that being tall or big boned as she called it wasn't the same as having hardened muscles. Besides, women in his village were strong from working so many hard hours, and he wouldn't be the one to negate their potential even if women did often think they were bigger than they were. Still, he could tire and might need their help rowing this mongrel. Even though he could have sworn it had shrunk, he still had never seen a dog as big as this one.

Eventually, they reached their boats. Together they were able to load the dog onto Nohm's boat. It felt easier than he originally thought it would be to lift it, so he wondered again if it had gotten even smaller or somehow could lighten itself. *No way, it is just a dog, a really amazing dog, but still just a dog. Now I'm really imagining things.* He almost shared his thoughts, but he thought for sure the girls would think he was going crazy.

When the dog whimpered, he worried that they moved it too much. He would do everything that he could to save the dog who had helped them, but he wasn't about to give up on his dream of being one of the first five back to the village, so he was determined to push himself to the brink to get there as fast as they could. *However, if you die,* he imagined talking to the dog in his head, *I won't hesitate to lighten my load into the middle of the waterway.* At that thought, Shadow seemed to look straight at him as if he understood what he was thinking. *That's just silly*, he said to himself while shaking his head and rowing with all his might towards home.

10

When Candade had asked Greecher if she could stop by her home to tell her mom they were going to the ceremony pit to see the village council, he had agreed to meet her there. She had no intention of going to the village council though. She had snuck into the house and taken some food and other supplies, and set out into the forest. That had been a couple of hours ago, and she hadn't stopped walking yet. She didn't know where she was headed, but she figured going north towards the mountains was as good a plan as any since that is the direction that Swish had flown when he left them. Her head was clouded with grief, so her decisions about where she went might have been clouded as well. She worried that Greecher or one of the other council members would come looking for her. Yet, she doubted that would happen. She thought that they would be too busy to worry about her with the winners of the Primitus arriving home soon. They would have to be there to facilitate the celebration and the next ceremony.

For a brief moment, her mind left her worries behind as she thought about the Primitus challenge and hoped Nohm was one of the first five. She felt bad that she wouldn't be there to welcome her friend back, but it couldn't be helped. She had to get as far away from the village as she could. Thankfully, when she had stopped at her cottage to get supplies, she found the herbs that helped her to sleep and brought them. It was a good thing that Lea had done what she asked. Now, she would just have to find a safe place to set up camp because it wouldn't be a good idea to use the herbs to sleep and not be aware of the dangers around her in the forest.

She had been walking for hours and hours when she decided to stop and rest. She wasn't sure where she was going, but she sensed that she needed to keep moving in a northern direction. She was already so tired. She didn't remember how slow and hard it was to walk such a long distance since she was used to flying high and fast on her dragon. Oh, how she missed her Swish. *Where was he and what was he doing?* How she prayed to the High God that he was okay. She found a rocky hill that would offer her protection from the back while she hoped that the fire she was building would protect her front. She was so tired and wanted to sleep. She wasn't sure she cared what happened to her anyway without her Swish. With the comfort of the fire to give her warmth in what was fast becoming bitter cold weather, and with the aid of the herbs that Benjess had given her, she closed her eyes and fell into an unfit sleep.

11

When Hopel and Little One finally made it back to the village, Candade was not there. All he could find out was that she had left instead of going to a council meeting after Swish had disappeared, and no one knew where she had gone.

The village was alive with anticipation since the Primitus challengers were beginning to return. Hopel knew the first challengers that had returned. Victor, who had turned sixteen in the fore year, was smart and strong, and he was known to have a kind heart because he often would help when there was need. It was not surprising that he had done well with his clever strength to lead him. Next, Sarai, the youngest in the competition, had arrived. That surprised Hopel more and he began to worry for his friends. If they didn't arrive soon, they might be eliminated. He wondered what was keeping them since they knew as much about the Whispering Forest as anyone could know since Lisbeth and Nohm's uncle had taught them. Plus, Hopel had shared everything that he had experienced in the fore year.

Do you think it is okay if we fly around a little to see who might be coming? Hopel asked his dragon.

No, I'm pretty sure we aren't supposed to do that. We are supposed to find out when everyone else does, she answered him. *Also, you do realize that the council will probably be calling us the first free chance they get, so since Candade isn't here anyway, I'm not sure we can keep what we saw a secret.*

Ugh. I guess you are right. I guess we will have to tell them what we saw, but before we do that, I'd still like to know how my friends are doing. What is the point of being able to fly if we aren't allowed to fly and see who is coming? It was a rhetorical question. He knew she wouldn't answer. Thus, he paced back and forth waiting impatiently.

It was in the midst of his pacing when he heard shouts from the village and someone ran by him hurriedly yelling something about a stretcher.

Oh, no. I hope no one is hurt. Just hearing the word "stretcher" brought back painful memories of his friend Natter's death the previous year. He was thinking in mind-speak, so he knew Little One understood how he felt.

Little One offered to fly him to where they saw the commotion, but it was a short distance, and he had a lot of nervous energy right now that he wanted to wear off, so he decided to run. Besides, he had been flying in the saddle for so long and his buttocks were so sore that he preferred the ground now for at least a little break. Also, he knew she would tell him if anything was wrong because she could fly to the council grounds where all the commotion was and where the challengers were arriving and communicate back to him in mind-speak.

He was one of the fastest runners in the village though and arrived only minutes after her, more refreshed and relaxed after his run. Boy, he was relieved at what he saw. The stretcher held a dog, not a person. His friends and another girl that he didn't recognize stood right beside it. They had made it. They were third, fourth, and fifth to arrive and would be allowed to climb the dragon cliffs to try to bond. He rushed towards his friends and was among the many to hug them and congratulate them. His friend, Nohm, managed to stop the onslaught of congratulatory friends, family, and acquaintances long enough that he could explain that the dog on the stretcher had saved them and needed help.

The other girl that accompanied his two friends also interjected, "Please," she looked around at the others, pushing through the crowd, "this dog saved our lives and we need to pull him to the healers now!" She grabbed the stretcher again and started in the direction of the healers. Nohm grabbed the other side to assist her.

As he watched his friends walk to the healers, Hopel felt someone bump into him. He hadn't realized that Benjess, the herbalist's son, was standing right next to him until he heard Benjess grumble, "All this commotion because they saved a mutt." As if annoyed at the interruption to his day, he turned around and started to walk away. Well, that was odd. Benjess was one of the shyest boys in the village, so why the attitude? He didn't remember him being anything but pleasant to people. Maybe Benjess was having a bad day or maybe Hopel was just imagining all of it. Hopel had a lot happen in the past that could have made him paranoid. Before he could turn and ask him anything, Benjess had disappeared. Probably, he went back to his shop, he thought as he shrugged. Oh well, if he got a chance, he would go ask him what he meant… but really, no big deal. He had more important things to worry about now and really after a few minutes, he didn't give it another thought.

12

With all the commotion in the village, Lea knew that they wouldn't miss her for a while. She had noticed Candade leaving the village, so she packed a sack herself and set out to follow her. She felt like her friend needed someone. The problem was that she didn't have a clue where Candade had gone. For some reason, she felt compelled to go to the dragon cliffs. Maybe she could climb it and see something from up there. Supposedly, it was a dangerous thing to do without proving yourself worthy, but she trusted the dragons. No normal dragon had ever hurt a human being. She didn't think they would mind if she climbed their cliff to look for her friend as long as she didn't bother any eggs, as if she would even see an egg. She wasn't planning on going that high up anyway, but she really felt like she needed to do this to look for Candade. At any rate, she was almost to the cliffs now, so no turning back. She would be brave.

When she finally arrived at the cliffs, she didn't even know where to begin climbing. She walked around under the cliffs and looked for a decent spot. Finally, she got a sense that she had found a workable place where the climb up didn't seem so difficult, when she started to have second thoughts again. She didn't even bring any safety equipment for climbing. That wasn't good. Her brother, Hopel, would be furious with her. People had been doing this for years, and they always had training and brought climbing equipment, he would say. Still, she couldn't seem to stop herself from trying. For some reason, she thought she felt compelled to climb right here at this very spot, and really, looking at it more closely now, it didn't even seem that steep. Thus, after warring within herself for a few brief moments, she began her climb.

After hiking for a while up the mountain on what seemed like an actual path, she grew tired and rested on a stone ledge. Looking to her left and right sides, the rocks were impossibly steep. It is good she didn't climb on those precipitous rocks, she thought. Still, she wondered why everyone said these cliffs were so hard to climb. You just had to find a good place to ascend. This spot certainly wasn't difficult, though the hike was good exercise. *Did she find the only walking trail on the whole mountain? Why would she find it while no one else ever had?*

It was about mid-sunstar in the day when, shivering, she estimated that she had been hiking for about five kilometers before it happened. She was just about to turn around because she really couldn't see much from where she had hiked, when she felt as if she heard a whisper. *Was someone up here?* Nervously, she started climbing again and then within only a few more moments of hiking, she thought she heard it again… a whisper… almost as if it was calling to her… in her innermost being. *Was it her imagination?* She was no longer nervous. In fact, she felt the opposite, and she was flooded with peace. *Yet, why wouldn't she be nervous?* She was always told that they were not allowed to do this, but here she *was* doing it, and that alone should have made her nervous, but now… now she felt… the best word that she could think of to describe it was… tranquility. Moving somewhat slowly now, she went around a bend where a bulging tree branch projected out onto what she thought was the path and seemed to end it on purpose, and that is where she spotted something under some brush. An egg! Yet, it was the most unusual egg that she had ever seen. Never before had she ever heard of an egg that looked like this one. It looked like… like… ice! *Why would dragons that breathed fire have an egg that looked like it was made out of ice? What was she even doing here looking at it? Was she supposed to be here?* Her tranquility vanished as she perused the sky looking for dragons. Maybe she really was doing something wrong.

For just a fleeting minute, the war within her started again and the peace that had flooded her only moments before left her as she tipped sideways and almost tripped over the branch. Looking over at it, she felt dizzy. The path, which should continue on the other side of the tree branch, was not even there. Instead, all she saw was a deep, impassable incline that was straight down for miles. She clutched the tree and was dizzy again. *Steady.* The whisper! She heard it again… or felt it… in her head, in her heart, in her soul. Was she going crazy? *No, you are all right and chosen. I'm real and I'm yours.* It felt like it was from the egg!

But, I'm not worthy to bond to a dragon egg. I'm too young and I haven't done the Primitus Challenge to prove myself. Was she speaking to it? She felt like it heard her. She stepped back to distance herself from it.

I say that you are, and that is all that matters. I am yours and you are mine. Then it was quiet. The peace was enough… still urging her to listen and obey.

I'm scared. What if I get in trouble from the council? I didn't earn this. She tried again to speak to the baby dragon that seemed to call out to her. She didn't want to reject… what most people felt was the most beautiful gift possible in this world, but she wanted, or needed, to explain how she was not worthy because she didn't do the first challenge and wasn't of age. This time the whisper was louder. *We say that you are.*

That was it. There was not another reply from the whispering voice. She still felt the peace, but she heard nothing further from the egg. She didn't need to hear anything further… the whispering voice had told her… *We say that you are…* and it was still resounding in her head, no in her entire being. She just knew that she should listen and obey. Thus, she pushed away the fear that was intent on destroying her purpose. She would not let fear win; instead, she believed and gathered the egg in her arms before descending the path.

13

Candade had been walking for days. She was now clear about what she needed to do in order to find Swish. Her troubling dreams in the fore nights had told her one thing. Something was calling her to Swish in the north. He must be there, and he must need her. Disturbing her the most was that her nightmares about Sanchezo kept reoccurring. The last dream was the most disturbing. The evil king was talking to something in the shadows that felt like pure evil. If that was the case, then he wasn't working alone. Well, she guessed she knew that because he had gotten his power and dark magic from somewhere or something. You couldn't force a bond with a dragon using light magic. Sanchezo forced bonds using dark, demon magic.

Anyway, she felt even more urgency to find Swish. She had no idea how she would make it on foot, but she would try or she would die. She wouldn't be apart from her bond any longer. Packing up her few belongings, her head still in a fog, she continued her hike towards the north. She was no longer worried about the council following her since she had been walking for days and hadn't seen anyone.

First item on her agenda today was to hunt for a meal. She could use her bow and arrow, but she didn't really feel like she had the energy, and either she had scared all the small animals away or there weren't any around this part of the woods today. Perhaps, she could find some berries to sustain her, but that would require more hunting and luck. *No, the easiest thing to do is to look for beetle grubs. Split their bodies open and toast them on what is left of the fire, and they really aren't that nasty,* she thought. In their village, children were all taught in school how to survive in nature. She didn't really understand why though since most of them never even left the village. Still, it was part of their education. She would also have to hunt for a mountain stream to collect some water. Yes, this would work. She would make it. There was no turning back now. *Swish, here I come.* She used their mind-speak even though she didn't think he heard her.

14

When Lea had left the mountain, she had glanced back and no longer could even see a path. It was like it hadn't even been there! What's more, right above where she had found the egg, she thought she glimpsed a gigantic, ethereal, pure white dragon on the cliffs spread shimmering wings and take off into the sky generating a gentle icy and if she dared say, peppermint scented, breeze to flow through her, sending a tingling shiver through out her body. She had never heard of such a magnificent dragon, and since the egg was so unusual, she wondered if it was the young dragon baby's real mother. After all, the mother dragons allowed their eggs to bond with a human. She shook her head as if to try and clear her vision. With the sunstar-light shining in her eyes, she really couldn't see that well, and maybe it had just been her imagination.

She was anxious to get back to the village, but she really was unsure what to do when she got there. What would she tell the council? *Who knows what they will say.* She hadn't had permission to do any of this, and the Primitus Challenge had just ended, which meant five Lexonite youths who did earn the right to climb the cliffs would be ready to start on this journey. Did she mess up one of their chances when this dragon chose her? *Would one less Lexonite who earned the right be given a dragon now?* Maybe she could hide the egg in the barn. No, that wouldn't work; she needed to protect the baby dragon while it was in the shell, and she couldn't do that if it wasn't next to her at all times. Her brother, Hopel, had taught her that. When it was older, they would protect each other, but right now that was all her responsibility, given to her by the wild dragons. No, it was just no use; she would have to be honest and go straight to the council.

When Lea finally returned to the village, it was alive with activity. Everyone was either bustling around in the market or at the ceremony where the council was probably proclaiming the winners of the Primitus. Unless she missed it, and the Primitus winners already left for the Secundus Challenge, which meant they were on their way to climb the dragon cliffs now.

Wow, she marveled again at what had occurred. In the past, climbing the cliffs was something she hadn't even planned to do; and yet, for seemingly no reason that she could understand, she had just felt compelled to do it and had found the egg. Hopel had told her how hard his climb up the mountain had been. He had definitely used his equipment to help him. She again wondered at the strange mountain path that seemingly had just been there for her. *Did it really just appear and disappear? How could that have happened?* Would anyone in the village believe her? Maybe that ethereal white dragon that she thought she glimpsed had used her magic to make it possible for her to reach this egg. She didn't know a lot about dragon magic, but she knew dragons used it rarely because it depleted them of strength and using too much could even kill them. That kind of magic would have taken an incredible amount of strength. She hoped if that mysterious wild dragon had been her new baby dragon's mother, that she still lived, and she again marveled at the extent she would have gone to give her… not even a child of age fifteen, which was the required age to try these challenges… this amazing and unique egg.

When Leah returned to the village, she held her head up high and headed straight for the village ceremony pit and the council. They might be busy, but this couldn't wait. As she walked through the crowd, she spotted her brother, Hopel, with Lisbeth and Nohmran, his two best friends. She noticed that they seemed deep in conversation over something, but upon hearing a plethora of gasps around them, they stopped their conversation and stared straight at her, mouths agape. What she didn't notice was that there were dozens of people just like them who were all staring at her as she walked past them. She acknowledged her brother with a nod, but she didn't stop. She kept walking towards the council. Behind her, a crowd began to follow.

When she arrived at the place where the council gathered to celebrate the winners of the Primitus, they turned and looked at her. For some reason, she sensed they already knew what had happened. They waited for her to speak though.

"Uh." she stammered softly. "I was called to be bonded." That pretty much summed it up, she figured, and she could barely get that out because she was so nervous, and being nervous and unable to talk was not in her normal nature.

The crowd began to murmur behind her seemingly getting angrier and angrier because everyone knew she hadn't done the challenge and most anyone could see that she wasn't of age if they didn't already know it.

She hadn't noticed that Hopel and his friends were directly behind her and formed a half circle around her in unspoken protection for her. It wouldn't have been necessary though because the dragon bonded on the council kept the crowd at a distance with a glance and an occasional growl.

Bocaj spoke first, which was what normally happened since he was the senior council member. "Lexonites, you will let this child speak." Then Rosata, his dragon-bond, growled to ensure they listened. "Tell us, child, what happened. Start from the beginning, and this time pick up your head and speak loudly." He stared directly into her eyes. The order he gave her was not to be denied.

So with her head held high and speaking clearly, she began to convey the whole story about how she had found the egg, but she didn't recount the fact that she had started out looking for Candade. She wouldn't bring her into this. She had to pause a few times at the surprised murmurs from the surrounding people until it grew quiet again, and then she proceeded to describe all that had happened.

When she finally finished, there wasn't a sound to be heard. The murmurs had died out and people stood and stared at her and the egg in awe. They could see that the egg was different than any they had ever seen before. Never before did they see an egg that looked like it was covered in pure ice, but since Lea was holding it they knew it mustn't be cold… at least not to her. The crowd eagerly awaited Bocaj's reply.

After speaking to his fellow council members, Bocaj finally spoke again. "It seems that for whatever reason, a dragon queen has chosen Lea to bond with her egg."

Gasps could be heard everywhere again, but no one's gasp was louder than Lea's as she covered her gaping mouth… that would explain the unusual egg. Despite her surprise, Lea was thankful that she did not hear one from her brother. Even that subliminal support gave her courage.

Bocaj continued, "Council member Uria and her dragon bonded Azra have volunteered to mentor Lea. Although unusual to our customs, we will not, no I mean we *cannot*, disallow what the dragon queen desires for her egg, and it is obvious by the occurrences that this is what she wants. We ask that you all return to the festivities because today is the day we honor the five and tomorrow they will begin their journey to the dragon cliffs. The bonding challenge for the five has not been changed by the extraordinary gift that was bestowed on Lea by the dragon queen. The five will still have their chance at becoming one of the bonded. Lea, Uria asks that you remain to discuss the beginning of your training."

As the crowd dispersed and went back to the festivities, Lea cautiously moved towards Uria and her dragon, Azra. She noticed that Hopel had stayed by her side, but upon seeing Uria motion him to go with the others, he reluctantly moved away also with a quick squeeze of the hand, something that was unusual between the two siblings.

15

Courtnia was at the healers with Shadow and was pleased when the healers told her that Shadow was doing really well and healing appropriately. She was exceedingly thankful that after they had looked at her arm, they took the time to care for him, since he was just a dog and being neither dragon nor human didn't make him really important in some people's eyes. However, the healers didn't even argue with her after she had relayed everything that had occurred in the Whispering Forest, and they seemed genuinely concerned for him when she shared how he had helped to save them from the Crotaw.

One of the lead healers, Xian, mentioned that even if Shadow hadn't saved them, they would never deny treatment to one such as he. Courtnia didn't understand at all what he meant by it, but Xian refused to comment further on it.

Instead, he informed her that he was Nohmran's and Lisbeth's uncle and asked her to tell him everything that had happened with all of them on their challenge.

At first she was surprised they were related. Most

Lexonites were dark in complexion like Xian, but Nohmran and Lisbeth shared red hair and a lighter complexion. In contrast, Xian's deep black hair was shoulder length, and tied back off his head, which allowed him to do his work more efficiently. Briefly, she reminisced on how some of the Lexonite villagers didn't think *she* was Lexonite enough to try the challenge. She thought they should have worried about Nohm and Lisbeth even *being* Lexonite seeing as how they were the only ones in the whole village with red hair, but she realized the thought was uncharitable and pushed it away. Nohmran and Lisbeth were definitely cousins with their hair and skin complexion, and apparently that didn't hold true for the rest of their family, but who cared. She didn't know where they got it, but it also didn't matter.

Looking at Nohmran's and Lisbeth's uncle now, she could easily make out the worry lines that deepened and aged his face because the beard on Xian was a mere shadow that didn't disguise his concern in the least. Even more notable to her were his deep brown eyes, which sparkled with humor when she shared with him the story of what had happened in the forest when she had joined the cousins on the challenge, and they had scared her by popping out behind a rock. Alternately, they filled with concern for Shadow and for all of them when she shared the events of the fight with the Crotaw. When she had finished telling him everything, she was completely surprised at herself for having shared so much. This was not like her, but there was just something about Xian that invited her to open up to him.

After she told him that Nohmran and Lisbeth were well and had made it as two of the first five, he breathed a sigh of relief, though the concern did not leave his eyes. She wasn't even sure he was really talking to her when he spoke aloud while examining Shadow, "I'm surprised a Crotaw attacked. These creatures from the dark have not been seen in a very long time, and they do not usually attack us, much less come up from the underground during the day. I wonder why it would come out of its hole to do such a thing."

Courtnia just shrugged her shoulders because she certainly had no idea. That's what Nohmran had said, but someone needed to tell the Crotaw that. As she watched Xian examine Shadow, she began to wonder if the dog had shrunk again. In fact, she was sure his eyes had been a brown color, but now the eyes that stared back at her were no longer brown, but instead they were a deep golden color with a mere sprinkling of brown flecks in them. She was going to mention it to Xian, when she decided against it. He would probably just think she was crazy… the idea that the dog's eyes changed colors… what was she thinking?

After thanking him for taking care of Shadow, she reluctantly left the healers to finish the ceremonies. She really didn't want to leave him for the pomp and circumstance of ceremonies, and she wished they were already over. While it was an honor, she was thoroughly exhausted and she knew that she needed to get a night's rest before she began her climb up the dragon cliffs. Xian promised to look after Shadow until her return. She wasn't sure what she would do with him anyway if she bonded because there was no way Shadow would keep up with her while she flew on a dragon's back, especially if they were sent on a mission.

As she walked back, she definitely noticed some commotion going on. People were calling out to her… something about how she needed luck because someone had already bonded. Now that was crazy since the winners didn't start out for the cliffs until the morrow, and she didn't see how it was possible that anyone had bonded without having won the Primitus. At any rate, she wasn't going to worry about that. When the ceremony ended, she would go home and rest until they began their trek to the dragon cliffs; that is, if she could rest because she was so excited for the morrow.

16

Hopel was surprised when he and Little One were summoned to the council grounds. He thought for sure they would be too busy to summon them for a while. At least, if he got it over with, he could report to them and then go look for Candade. Nohm had made him promise to go look for her when Hopel had told him what they saw in the northern mountains. Since Nohm and Lisbeth had to do the Secundus and climb the cliffs, this time Nohm wouldn't be able to go himself. Hopel knew how much he cared about Candy. The decision not to follow her now must really be hurting him.

He doubted Candy would want that anyway. Though everyone knew she had mutual feelings for him, she wasn't ready to admit it yet since Nohm had been friends with her kid brother their whole lives before Taylor killed him while working with Sanchezo to bond with Natter's dragon, and seeing Nohm as anything but her kid brother's friend was difficult at best for her.

At the council meeting, Hopel reported what he had seen to everyone present, which included only bonded members of the village and their dragons because only bonded Lexonites and their dragons could be on the council. Bocaj, the head of the council, was the one to begin questioning him as usual. His humongous caramel and moss camouflaged dragon, Rosata, was next to him. They didn't waste time and immediately asked him what they had seen on their mission to the north.

When Hopel reported that very little life was thriving in the northern lands, the council was definitely concerned. They understood that despite the cold, there was a population of animals that usually still thrived there, and Hopel and Little One hadn't seen any sign of them, which was not normal. They were even more concerned when they heard that they had spotted Sanchezo in the cave with some very strange and deadly looking creatures. Despite Little One urging him to do so, Hopel didn't tell the council that he saw Swish in the cave with Sanchezo too. What he did tell them was that they saw a different dragon than Cordo, and of course they'd seen Cordo too with Sanchezo. He was very lucky because they didn't push him for more details. They assumed Hopel and Little One didn't know the dragon since he didn't tell them a name, he guessed, and it wasn't exactly fibbing if he just left out a few things. Little One growled at this when he told her in mind-speak.

At any rate, the council was troubled. They thought Sanchezo had managed to get another dragon using his dark magic, and if he could acquire another dragon, who knows how many he could get or what army he could build, especially since he also seemed to be doing something to the northern animals.

When Hopel told them about the red glowing stone that mesmerized the dragons almost as if it put them in a trance, they seemed even more distressed. He knew they were talking in mind-speak and he couldn't hear them, so he asked Little One if she could hear them.

I'm a new dragon, so I haven't learned everything yet either, but they are not closing me off from hearing what they are saying in mind-speak. This is probably because I am a dragon and it concerns me. From what I can gather and understand, there is a legend that a special stone exists. The dragon queens throughout the centuries imbued their magic into it. The elders seem to believe that when a queen is old and their spirit will soon pass into the next realm, they sacrifice the remaining years of their life to give us their remaining magic. It is a gift that only the queens can do and they do it to ensure that this particular light magic will stay in our world to guide the other dragons. The stone is supposed to remain hidden on the dragon cliffs. They can't imagine that Sanchezo would have been able to find it. Also, if it is true that he somehow did find it, they have no idea of all the potential harm he could do with it. They are afraid that he could somehow twist it with dark magic and control dragons with it. They wonder if this is why a dragon queen let one of her eggs bond with Lea. Usually future queens do not bond, but perhaps the human bond is a protection of sorts.

Well, I would agree with that if we hadn't seen Swish there. Being bonded with Candade didn't protect him, Hopel replied.

Well, maybe it is different for queens. Perhaps the bond offers a deeper protection with a queen that extends to the other dragons and dragon bonded. Losing any dragon to Sanchezo is dangerous, but losing a queen and then more dragons as a result of losing a queen… Her voice trailed off as if it was too scary to even entertain the thought, and he didn't need her to finish it to understand how bad that would be.

After they were finally dismissed from the council meeting, Hopel decided that he was going to stop by the herbalist adobe to talk to Benjess before he went home. Little One went hunting, so now was as good a time as any. He wondered if he could find out what had been bothering Benjess when his friends had returned from the Primitus Challenge. He also thought he could see if he knew anything about Candade because he knew that lately, since the kidnapping, she was going there for herbs to help her sleep, and Lea had told him that she did this right before disappearing too.

It was just as he was about to enter through the door of the herbalist's shop when he thought he heard arguing inside. Pausing and leaning his ear on the door, he waited to see if he could hear who might be arguing. Unfortunately either the door was thicker than expected, or they stopped arguing. Since he was unable to hear anything further, he went in.

His eyes adjusted to the dark rather quickly. This is something he noticed occurred since bonding with Little One. Benjess stood behind the counter, and Hopel tried not to look shocked when he saw that Benjess had a large bruise on his left eye. Beside him stood Benjess' father, Breker, whom Hopel hadn't seen for weeks. Hopel looked directly at Benjess when he asked, "Is everything okay? I thought I heard arguing before I came in."

Breker didn't give Benjess a chance to respond though, "I don't believe that is any of your business even if it wasn't your imagination… which it was. Benjess just had an accident and fell with one of the herb bottles." He motioned with his head for Benjess to get the broom sitting in the corner to clean up the mess, and Benjess skulking moved away to comply. "Is there something that you wanted, Hopel?" His voice was anything but friendly when he asked.

Hopel tried to smile although he was afraid it came out as more of a grimace. "My friend, Candade, is missing." Hopel then turned to Benjess again. "It is my understanding that you spoke to her before she left, Benjess. I am wondering if you know anything about this?"

"He doesn't and if you aren't going to buy anything, we have things we need to do," Abruptly, Breker answered for him again.

Hopel, with clenched fist and through gritted teeth responded, "Well, *thank you* for your *help* then. I guess I will be going," but when he turned to leave, he walked out slowly. Despite his slow departure, to get across whatever point he was trying to make, he guessed that if he had stayed even a minute longer, he might have regretted it and said something that he shouldn't say out of anger. He pondered as he started to walk more quickly back through the village, *The nerve of that guy. He wouldn't even let his son talk.* It was bad enough that he had a bruised eye, but why should Breker care if he asked him about his friend? Plus, if he was acting like that, he couldn't be too worried about customers buying from him. Something didn't add up.

17

Courtnia was hiking towards the dragon cliffs when the craziest thing happened. She could have sworn that she saw Shadow following her. She didn't think that was possible because she had just left him with the healers on the fore day. At any rate, when she had called him, nothing responded, so she decided that she must have imagined it and continued on towards the cliffs. This time, she didn't see any of the other five challengers from the village, and she wasn't planning on joining forces with them again either way. There was no need because they couldn't work together for this challenge, and she preferred to be alone anyway. Still, she did wonder how the others were doing and if they had reached the cliffs yet. After all, they had helped her when the Crotaw attacked her, and they helped her to save Shadow too.

Now, nearing the cliffs, she grew excited. This was everything that she had dreamed about for as long as she could remember. She was awestruck when she looked at the majestic cliffs. Usually, you could see dragons flying high above them or resting on the steeper cliffs, but today there were none. It was an odd occurrence that the dragons didn't seem to be around on the days when the challengers climbed the cliffs. She knew it wouldn't matter if the dragons were on their cliffs since the dragons wouldn't harm them, so she wondered why they seemed to disappear on these days… or at least that is what she'd heard, and it must be true because she didn't see a single dragon here today. Well, maybe there were some dragons here, and she just didn't see them because she knew dragons could practically make themselves invisible, or some dragons could. In fact, they would never leave their eggs unprotected, so they had to be here somewhere. With that comforting thought, she found a spot to rest for the night. She wanted to be fresh for the climb the following day. She could see a fire in the distance and guessed that one of the other challengers had already made camp for the night, and she wondered if she should join them, but then decided against it. It wouldn't do for her to rely on these people too much. Thus, she built a fire and made her camp as far away as possible while staying near the cliffs.

Courtnia awoke to the strangest scene. Shadow, resting at her feet, stared straight at her. "What? How did you get here?" She thought she still must have been imagining things because he looked different again. His fur was darker now and was almost as black as midnight, and he seemed to have grown again and was almost as tall as a small pony. She just shook her head to get rid of the crazy thoughts.

"I guess you are feeling better, but how in the world did you find me and catch up to me?" She asked him aloud, though of course she wasn't expecting him to talk back to her. The funny thing is that she got the feeling that he was trying to talk to her. He nuzzled her hand and made some strange whining sounds that sounded almost human like.

She was surprised when she felt like he was communicating his feelings to her… his feelings of being happy to see her anyway. Well, she guessed that was true with any dog. You knew they were happy to see you when they wagged their tail, but Shadow didn't do anything. He just laid still, staring at her, and didn't even move a paw, except to occasionally nuzzle her hand, but she still could sense his feelings of being happy to see her. This was really strange. "You know what?" She told him aloud again. "I don't think I am imagining it either. I think I feel what you feel." This time his body shook excitedly. "Wow, people are really going to think me nuts now. Then again, what people? It isn't like I talk to anyone." She patted his head, and then packed up her belongings, so she could begin her hike up the mountain. "Well, Shadow, I got to go, but you can stay here and wait if you like."

Shadow watched her. After she was done putting everything in her pack, he started pacing around her nervously.

"What is it, boy?" She asked him. "I can't stay here with you. I have to get moving." Instead of moving away from her though, he pushed against her, almost knocking her down. "Shadow! Watch out." She yelled at him.

It didn't seem to faze him, and he refused to move out of her way. Then, he started nudging her backwards away from the cliffs. "Are you crazy? Move. I only have today to find a dragon egg to bond…" She couldn't finish her sentence because he shoved her back again. She wouldn't hurt him even if she could, so she began to get anxious when he wouldn't move and let her approach the cliffs. It was almost as if he didn't want her to climb the cliffs! She neared tears and tried to plead with him. "Shadow, I've been waiting to bond my whole life. Why are you preventing me from climbing the cliffs?" She wasn't able to move around him either because as soon as she sidestepped, so would he, blocking her again. Also, unbelievably, he seemed to have grown again. When he first appeared, he seemed to be shoulder height, but now, she could have sworn he was as tall as she was. "Why are you doing this to me? I should have left you in that forest." She felt a pang of remorse as soon as she said it. It felt wrong, but she was growing angrier by the minute. The odd thing was that Shadow seemed to be growing angrier too as if she should understand what he was trying to tell her, but didn't, and it frustrated him.

It was right then that he began to shift in shape. Her eyes grew large and her mouth dropped. Right in front of her, he was morphing into what looked like a rhinoceros, only three times the normal size, almost as big as a dragon, with wings and black armored scales on its sides. This creature had longer legs than a rhinoceros too. She imagined that despite the weight, it could run fast with those long legs and probably didn't even need to fly. "Whaaat… she stuttered, barely getting it out… are you?"

Almost as if he was aware that he was scaring her, he morphed back into a dog and rubbed against her leg. "Dogs and dragons… um, don't do that. You can't be either of them?" He, of course, didn't answer her. He laid back down into his original position on the ground and just stared at her again.

"You're not going to let me bond are you?" As soon as she said it, she felt him relax and a feeling of happiness and contentment was relayed to her again. She sank to her knees and cried silently. She had waited her whole life to bond with a dragon, and for some reason, Shadow did not want her to climb the cliffs and try, and she had no idea what was going on. After a while, she dried her tears and stood. This was just her luck, but she was not the kind of person that would cry for long since it didn't do any good. She decided to walk back to the village and see if she could find Xian.

He seemed to know something about Shadow when she was there. Perhaps he could tell her what was going on.

"You know if you could get that big, you could have helped more with the Crotaw and got hurt less," she said as she glared at him and started to walk back to the village with Shadow weaving in and out of the forest behind her. Even as she said it though, somewhere deep down she knew that he didn't want anyone but her to see him change or to suspect how unusual he really was.

18

Nohm worried for his friend Candade as he climbed the cliffs. He knew Hopel would go look for her, but he wished that he could help. Distractedly, he pondered on how Lisbeth was doing as well. They had gone their separate ways ages ago because you had to climb the cliffs alone wherever you felt called to climb. While he knew his cousin was capable, he still worried about her. Although alluring and majestic, these cliffs were dangerously steep, and he hoped she was okay.

Besides, one thing he knew was that beautiful, dazzling things could be incredibly dangerous as well. The Strawthorn Field was a good example of that. He remembered how beautiful and enticing it looked but had they been pricked by one thorn, they would have died. Heck even a regular rose could hurt you with a sharp prick if you tried to pick one of its beautiful flowers. Yes, we often had to be careful with beautiful things. Beauty can be quite deceiving. Although perhaps the deeper lesson of the rose is that we need to accept the suffering hardship of the thorns to gain the reward of the beauty and aroma of the rose…

just like in life. He chuckled to himself. This mountain was making him a philosopher. Hopel would say he didn't think past what he was going to eat at his next meal. See, his friend had no idea how deep he could be.

He looked around him. He had actually climbed quite far while he was daydreaming about beauty and danger… funny, he should probably be paying more attention. There was a whole other line of thinking for him to delve into… the danger in daydreaming while climbing mountains, and here he was worrying about his cousin being careful. He chuckled to himself again. Funny how our mind wanders when we are bored.

Interrupting that line of thinking before it could get started, something nudged him. Well, he wouldn't exactly say nudged. It felt as if something else was speaking to his innermost being… indeed, at that moment, even chuckling with him. He got the sense that this very thing that he was hearing deep in his soul was calling to him and directing him. He grew excited and hopeful as he moved towards it.

Lisbeth was climbing back down the mountain with the most beautiful dragon egg that she had ever seen. Praising the Creator for her good fortune, she marveled at its beautiful aquatic, greenish-blue colors. She still had the sense of peace she'd felt when she heard the dragon egg calling to her. She knew they would be great friends for the rest of their lives… well, more than friends. Friends did not describe what bonding was. She didn't know if there was a word to describe feeling like you were one with a being, deep in your soul, yet separate as well. And she knew the feeling only deepened over time with the work they would put into their relationship. She would protect him and he would protect her as well. She didn't know how she knew it was a he, but she did. At the bottom of the mountain, Nohm was waiting for her, his face was glowing, and she knew immediately that he had bonded as well. What a glorious day!

19

When Courtnia reached the village, the first thing that she did was seek out Xian. Shadow had disappeared at the village boundaries. She didn't know what that was about. She tried to ignore the stares from the villagers as she passed by them. She could just imagine what they were thinking. They were probably feeling pity for her when they didn't see an egg, or worse, they probably thought that she was inferior and that there was something wrong with her because no dragon had chosen her. Well, the joke's on them, she didn't even get to try thanks to Shadow. Who knew, maybe there was something wrong with her if Shadow kept her from trying to bond. At any rate, she had to remind herself again that she didn't care what other people thought about her.

At the healers, when she asked for Xian, they didn't seem that anxious to help her. Looking at this large boned girl carrying her intimidating and dangerous whip with her for no apparent reason and looking completely healthy, they couldn't imagine what she wanted with any healer. She waited, for what felt like hours, while she thought that they went to look for him. Finally, one of the lead healers,

Wianda, arrived to let her know that he was not even there. Courtnia pondered how this apparently fragile, short, thin elderly woman with a cat that followed her everywhere was a leader of anything. She certainly didn't meet with Courtnia's expectation of how strong a woman should be. "Is there something that I can help you with?" Wianda asked when Courtnia still hadn't spoken.

Courtnia debated sharing with her what had happened, but finally decided against it. She had already shared the story of what happened in the forest with Xian when she brought Shadow to the healers, and she felt like she shouldn't be telling anyone else about the crazy stuff that happened around Shadow. Even more insane was that she felt like Shadow didn't want her to tell anyone else. Sighing, she answered a curt, "no," and left in search of him, herself.

20

Candade hadn't rested well the night before and despite the fire, she was extremely cold this far north. Usually, it was Swish that kept her warm in the cold temperatures. She was just about to put out her fire, when she turned around and saw them. It was about fifteen of the strangest creatures that she had ever seen in her life. At one time, they must have been normal animals, but they weren't anymore for sure. What she could have imagined was once a beautiful white fox, now was twice its normal size with fangs that almost touched the ground and dripped with saliva. *What in the world happened to it?* Next, she noticed an incredibly ugly white rabbit that was three times its normal size with humongous, saliva-dripping fangs and red eyes. That was only the beginning. Other creatures that someone or something must have perverted nature to create also began to surround her.

This debased corruption of nature almost made it impossible for her to recognize the beautiful animals that the Creator had intended. Obviously dangerous, they evoked fear just looking at them. It was bad enough that they were coming at her from land, but when she looked up, she was even more disheartened. Above her, swarmed a dark mass of purplish-black bees, each the size of a squirrel. There must have been fifteen of these flying creatures as well.

She quickly grabbed her sword. Looking behind her at the rock she had used for protection from attack at her rear, she knew that she was in trouble. She could try, but there was no way that she would be able to hold them all off without help… without her dragon… there were just too many.

She tried to stir up the fire again with a nearby stick, but as soon as she moved significantly, the bees began to swarm near her. *The fire must be holding the other creatures away, at least for now*, she thought briefly. As the first bee creature attacked her, she drew her sword up swiftly and cut its head off completely, which was easier than she thought since it was so big.

Even amidst the struggle, she was able to have some satisfaction that whoever created these things did it in error because the size would make them easier to kill. The size also kept them from all attacking her at once. *Funny, a regular swarm of bees attacking her would have been worse because they could have swarmed her at once*, she contemplated, even as she was fighting them, cutting the legs off one of the creatures that neared her left side.

"They thought to improve on the Creator's beings to bring destruction… I don't think so," she didn't realize that she yelled that aloud as she cut the wings off the second attacker on her right.

To her dismay, the creature that she had cut the legs off of somehow survived and was still trying to kill her. Now, the disgusting half-cut bee-like creature was sliding on the ground towards her, blood dripping from its belly. Sickened by the distorted being, she realized, dejectedly, that she would never be able to fight a second time against one of these nasty creatures. She just wouldn't have time when the next attacker was already upon her. Although severely injured, it wouldn't die, and it was insanely and persistently still trying to sting her from the ground while the others flew above her and also attacked. *I will have to be more careful to make the blow from my sword count*, she thought as she sliced the next one in the air and then spun towards the one now crawling close to her, and sliced its head off, which finally killed it. She then spun around just in time to avoid another one flying from above and closing in on her head.

After she had hacked through about half of the flying creatures, she realized the fire had been dying out and the land creatures were slowly inching forward. She was also tiring and knew she wouldn't last much longer. She offered up a silent prayer, but even as she did it, she fought within herself against a hopelessness that she was afraid would negate her silent prayer.

Even in the midst of her battle, her final thought and prayer before she focused completely on the fight was for her Swish. She prayed for his freedom and safety. If this was to be her last breath, and she couldn't somehow help him, she prayed the Creator would somehow save him.

21

Hopel and Little One had been flying for hours now, searching for Candade. Another great thing about having a dragon is that they were great trackers since they could see the tiniest objects miles away.

Periodically, Little One thought he saw evidence of her, and they would land and look for evidence of a campfire or proof that someone had been there recently. He was pretty sure that they were on the right track, and both of them felt an urgency to hurry though they didn't know why. Thus, they were flying as late into the night and as early in the morning as they were capable of, barely staying at their camp, and barely taking the time to eat. Hopel was beginning to feel guilty for waiting in Lexonite so long before starting his search. If anything happened to her, he doubted Nohm would forgive him too quickly, and the feeling in his gut told him that they needed to hurry. Little One was sure that the Creator was urging them to move faster. They were exhausted, but they kept moving at the fastest pace their bodies would allow.

Suddenly, he heard Little One roar loudly as she dived

down towards the forest. "Little One, what is it?" he asked her.

There was no time for her to answer, and really she didn't need to answer because in a matter of seconds, Hopel was able to see for himself. "What in the…?" Candade was on the ground fighting a hoard of creatures that surrounded her. She was obviously tiring though, and the creatures were getting closer.

"Little One, attack the flying creatures first, so she can at least focus on the land creatures," Hopel told his dragon though again there was no need because she was already roaring and breathing fire into the air above Candade's head.

Candade, her heart exceedingly thankful when she saw them, ducked to avoid being hit by the fire, rolling on the ground and coming up using her sword all at the same time to slice at the nearest ground creature.

Hopel had also jumped off of Little One when she neared the ground, rushing to Candade's side, to attack the creatures on the ground. With both of them attacking, it was only a matter of time before they would defeat the aberrations, which was good because there wasn't enough room for Little One to land and help since Candade had situated her camp close to the surrounding rock and trees for protection. Hopel knew Little One would watch from above them and make sure there were no more flying creatures as they both attacked by land. Although, occasionally, she was able to target a ground creature with her fire when the creature wandered a little further away from them. Still, she had to be careful because she didn't want to burn down the forest. Dragons usually hunted their prey in more open land, and they used their strong jaws and claws, not their fire to make the kill, especially when in more congested areas such as this one that was filled with trees and hills, so Hopel and Candade would have to do most of the fighting themselves.

In the midst of all the fighting, Hopel somehow observed that Candade's campfire was just dwindling away, which he realized meant that they had arrived just in time. A moment later, and Candade would have been lost to them.

He was fighting the brunt of the creatures now, fresh as he was, because she had tired and looked injured. She had cuts and bruises over almost every inch of her body. Though he didn't know if that was from this fight or another. He gestured and she moved more behind him to try to recuperate her strength and to defend any weak areas around him where an attacker might slip through.

Finally, as the last creature slithered towards them, Hopel's sword sliced through its middle and ended the attackers once and for all. Hopel was shocked that they hadn't run away when it was obvious that they were going to lose, but the creatures seemed intent on killing Candade regardless of whether they would live or not. Someone had imbued this single desire or destructive purpose into these creatures, and it was as essential to them as eating and breathing was to him, he guessed, because he had never seen such blind persistence in any animal. For sure, the desire to kill her was so strong that they were ignoring the pain that they must have felt after being injured in their efforts to get to her and destroy her.

Now, Hopel and Candade would have to figure out why someone was so intent on killing her that they sent this fearsome brood of deformed creatures.

"Aren't you getting tired of rescuing me?" Candade got the words out with difficulty, trying to make light of the situation though she was breathing hard, sweat pouring down her face, and fell exhaustedly to the ground.

Hopel reiterated the mood in kind, "Well, I don't think

Nohm would forgive me if I let anything happen to you," he smiled. Besides, didn't you and Swish rescue all of us from Taylor and Sanchezo last time? I guess we owe you."

"Hardly, it was a group effort and you know it," she told him between breaths.

"Well, okay then, I guess friends rescue each other at different times... let's leave it at that," he told her. She nodded tiredly, and he continued, "Now, I guess we better see to those wounds. It is a good thing dragon-riders carry around a healer's kit in their saddles. Greecher always said that we would never know when we would need it."

Candade winced guiltily when he spoke of Greecher. It just reminded her that she had left the village without permission. Luckily, Hopel would just guess it was from physical pain and spare her the embarrassment of explaining the grimacing facial expression.

22

Courtnia had already been through the whole village and wasn't able to find Xian. The only place that she had left to check was the herbalist shop. She knew it was uncommon for healers to go in there since they usually found their own herbs. Perhaps if it was something extraordinary that they needed and couldn't find it soon enough, they might shop there, but it wasn't often. Oh well, she figured it was worth a try.

When she entered, she scrunched up her nose. She sure didn't like the smell of this dark, dingy shop, and the crowded, dusty shelves were making her sneeze uncontrollably.

"Do you need something for that cold?" a voice asked.

Turning, she saw it was the herbalist's son, Benjess. She remembered seeing him before in the village. He didn't look so good now. He had a big bruise on one of his eyes. She wondered if he didn't need to do something to help himself first before he sought to help others.

"I don't. I'm just looking for someone," she answered a little more curtly than she probably should have.

"Well, that seems to be the game of the day," he replied.

"Wait, aren't you one of the five? Where is your egg? Didn't you bond?"

Courtnia wasn't surprised that he knew that she had been one of the chosen "five". The whole village always knew after the ceremonies and celebrations who the five chosen were. Ignoring his question, she growled her response, this time not caring about her harsh tone, "Have you seen Xian?"

He pretended not to hear her tone and ignoring her question now, he replied, "How badly did you want to bond?"

"What kind of question is that? Do you think I would have risked my life in the Whispering Forest if I hadn't wanted to bond?" She was getting even more irritated. Why didn't he just answer her question? She hoped he wasn't implying that she didn't bond because she didn't want it enough.

"Well, I have not seen Xian," he said finally, "but if you really want to bond, I might still be able to help you with that. I might know of someone else you could talk to that could help you," his less than sincere smile while he was saying it made her uneasy.

"Why would I want to see someone just because I didn't bond?" *What was he implying? There was only one way to bond. Wait… when she returned home from the challenge… didn't she hear that some young girl had bonded without going to the forest to do the challenge?* After thinking about it, she couldn't help herself and asked, "What do you mean?"

"Well, if you really still want to bond with a dragon, I've heard that there are other ways, and this person could help you with that, but of course, you couldn't tell anyone about this conversation," he said calmly.

Courtnia didn't feel calm. She knew that this was really odd, and she definitely should tell someone about it, and she should really scram out of there right away, but really who would even believe her? Everyone still looked at her like she was some kind of outsider. Besides, for some reason, curiosity got the better of her. "Who? Who is it and how?"

"I'm sorry. That I can't tell you until you decide this is something that you want to do, and only then will I set up a meeting."

"Uh, I'll have to think about it," was all she said.

"Well, you better not take too long. The offer expires after today," he said, and turned away to work on whatever substances he was shelving.

Without another word, she backed out of the door to leave.

Turning around, she bumped into Xian. "I heard you were looking for me," the tall dark man said as he rubbed his beard with a questioning look on his face.

"Um yes," Courtnia answered, shocked at seeing him so abruptly after all the time that she had spent looking for him. She wondered how he had found her instead.

"Well? Are you going to speak or not?" he asked, chuckling.

"Do you think we could go someplace more private?" she asked as she glanced back at the herbalist shop. She didn't know why, but she felt as if someone watched her here.

"Sure, let's take a walk, and we can talk while we walk," he replied.

Courtnia was not surprised when she realized that Shadow once again followed them. Xian also noticed and smiled.

"Well, I am just going to say it," Courtnia tried not to mumble because she knew what she was about to say sounded crazy. "Shadow changes size and shape. He can even change colors. While that sounds crazy and cool, what wasn't cool is that he followed me to the cliffs, and he kept me from trying to bond with a dragon. He kept pushing against me and forcing me back." In her own head, it sounded like she was making excuses, and she didn't want it to sound like she was making excuses and have him assume that she was a coward who was too scared to climb the cliffs. Thus, taking a deep breath, she explained further. "I mean that he really and physically wouldn't let me climb the cliffs. He changed into a creature much bigger than me and pushed me away from the mountain."

"What did he say?" Xian asked.

"Say?" Maybe Xian was crazier than her.

"Yes, *say*. You have bonded with a changeling, so I imagine you can hear him," he answered.

"What... I've done what? What is a changeling?" she stuttered in surprise and spoke quickly.

"I am somewhat astonished that he didn't explain."

"That's because I haven't bonded with anything. This dog or creature or whatever it is, just kept me from bonding with a dragon. It didn't *say* anything."

Xian shook his head as if disappointed in her. "A dragon isn't the only creature we bond with. Even rarer, and maybe even more of an honor because a changeling is thought to be even more ancient than a dragon, is when some of us are chosen to bond with a changeling. There is no ceremony for it. A changeling is not something you can look for since it can't be found unless it wants to be found. They find us, not vice-versa. If you looked around the village, you might not ever know who has bonded with a changeling because unlike dragon bonding, it is kept a secret, and a changeling can have many forms that might include animals you know or even animals you don't know."

Courtnia remembered the weird animal that Shadow turned into at the cliffs. It was definitely something that she had never seen before. "Why? Why would anyone keep it a secret if it is such a great honor instead of an embarrassment?"

"Because a changeling in its purest and true form is quite vulnerable to danger. They would be easier to hunt down and kill if we knew where they were, and knowing who they are bonded to would make them easier to find. In fact, that might be one reason it is unusual for them to bond. Also, until he feels that you have truly accepted your bond, he will probably not show his true form to even you. This might be why you are not clearly hearing him either."

"What? This is crazy! I didn't ask to bond with anything but a dragon." HE might say it was an even bigger honor, but all she felt were the whispers from people who would say that she wasn't good enough to bond with a dragon. This wasn't possible. All her life growing up people had made fun of her for the way she looked and for her status in the village. She had worked so hard to bond with a dragon, and now it was for naught. Turning to look at Shadow, she yelled at him. "Go away!" Even as she did it, she felt it was wrong. Then she ran away from both Shadow and Xian. At first she ran in no particular direction, but then she decided where she needed to go.

23

Uria and Azra extended Lea's class time on lessons about the history of dragon care. Lea was really growing tired of the lessons and wanted to go home early today. Even entertaining her younger siblings would be better than history lessons. Her stomach was also growling, and she was really looking forward to her mama's soup.

"Lea, will you pay attention? It is precisely your mishap this morning that makes these lessons necessary," Uria growled at her, mumbling about how Lea was too young for this.

Lea blushed, remembering the morning's incident. She hadn't tried it, but she had healed a dying hoopoe, and Uria had caught her. It was something that she didn't even know that she could do. In fact, she had never seen anyone do it. She wasn't even touching her egg at the time. She just saw the bird and felt sorry for it, and told her dragon egg that she wanted it beautiful and healthy again.

Lea, trying to hide her blush, remembered Uria's words from earlier today. According to Uria, it was because her baby dragon, even in its shell, was a queen. She said that queens had more magic, but that didn't mean they should use it. Uria wasn't even sure the baby dragon knew how dangerous it was to use magic. Even if her magic was from the Creator, it could still weaken her if she used too much. She droned on for what felt like hours about how it was part of Lea's responsibility to keep her dragon egg safe and to know these things. She explained how the two of them must have agreed on the healing magic since they were bonded or it wouldn't have happened. Her words exactly, "Gifts from the Creator need to be discerned and can't just be used 'willy-nilly'. It puts the dragon and dragon bonded and maybe even others in danger if used wrongly. Making sure that it is the will of the Creator, and not just the bonded, is important to keeping the magic in the light. Plus, everyone knows using magic weakens the dragon, and yours is just a baby."

Lea didn't know what she meant by "keeping the magic in the light", but she didn't want to ask either when Uria was in such a mood, and then she was also afraid to even open her mouth because she almost giggled when she thought of Uria's use of the words "willy-nilly". Though she quickly collected herself when Uria gave her *the look.* It wouldn't do to make Uria any angrier with her.

She had to promise Uria repeatedly not to wish, even in her mind, to her baby dragon for any magic, for any reason, before Uria finally let her go home. Clutching the pack in front of her that held her egg, she struggled to make her way home. She probably wasn't as strong as the other bonded since she was so young, so carrying her heavy charge was sometimes difficult, but since dragon eggs weren't fragile, the bonded never went anywhere without their egg and that included lessons. Besides, protecting them aside, in the formative stage, it was supposed to deepen the bond to keep them close at all times.

24

"You know Candade, you aren't in any condition to go looking for him. You are hurt, and something is still after you apparently." Hopel had spent what felt like forever arguing with her over returning back to the village instead of searching for Swish.

"I'm not going back without Swish, and if what you told me is true, then I'm going to have to sneak into that cave to reach him. When he sees me, I know he will snap out of it... just like last time. You, however, should go back because it isn't safe. We don't need Sanchezo capturing you too." Candade refused to be swayed. She didn't admit it to Hopel, but she was scared to death of being captured. She doubted the evil Sanchezo would let her live this time since the last time he had kidnapped her he had tortured her. Since that didn't work to force her to join him, she doubted that he would try again to turn her. This time, if he captured her again, she expected that he would kill her. In fact, she expected that he was already trying to kill her, which is why the deformed animals were attacking her. According to Hopel, he had Swish. He must be trying to break their bond, so he could force bond him to someone else.

"Well, he is using some kind of magic to hold him that he didn't have before… some kind of dragon stone. It is more dangerous to try to free him now. We should at least go back and tell the council," he pleaded. "You know I didn't tell them because I wanted to tell you first, but I should have told them."

"Yeah, because they were so much help last time," she snapped sarcastically. She felt bad though because she didn't want him to get in trouble because of her. Yet, she wasn't going to rely on them. "I will rescue my dragon or die trying and no one will stop me."

"You are being stubborn. The council did come to help us last time…"

Before he could go on, she interrupted him; "You mean they finally came… after they let him torture me for a month. I don't think I'll trust them to help us this time."

"Candade, that isn't what happened. You aren't thinking clearly…" At that comment, she turned her back on him, and walked away to lie down by the fire to sleep for the night. Hopel stopped talking. He didn't know what to do. He couldn't let her go in search of Swish alone. For one thing, it would take forever for her to find the cave even if she felt Swish's connection pulling her there because she would have to walk the whole way if Little One didn't fly them both. Besides, he doubted she would survive the bitter cold walk or be able to make the climb to the cave. The other reason was that Nohm would kill him if he let her go alone. Thus, exhausted from the earlier fight with the warped creatures, he lay down near the fire as well to try to sleep… even though he doubted he would be able to sleep on the hard ground.

25

Courtnia was told by Benjess to wait at the edge of the village for whomever she was supposed to meet at sunstar down. He seemed surprised when she had returned to the shop. Now, as she sat here waiting, she wondered again if she was doing the right thing. Xian said she already had an honored bond. There must be a reason that Shadow had chosen her, right? Still, what was the point of having a bond that she could not fly and hunt with? What was the point of having a bond when no one else even knew that she was bonded? She knew in Lexonite, status in the village, and jobs, really depended on whether or not you were bonded, unless you were lucky enough to own your own shop like Benjess. She didn't have that kind of money though, so she needed a dragon.

She raised her head when she heard the strangest chirp come out of a bird perched on a branch above her head. It was the most unusual little bird that she had ever seen. Really, it was beautiful, silver and gold tipped wings, tiny piercing eyes that almost looked intelligent and a gold tipped beak. Now, it made a chirping sound that almost sounded like it was "tsk, tsking" her as if it understood and disapproved of her thoughts.

Remembering what Xian had said about changelings being able to shape shift into many different shapes, she wondered if it could be Shadow. *Still, why in the world would he shift into such a puny, fragile thing like a bird? No, it couldn't possibly be him.* "Shoo," she shouted aloud at the bird. It just chirped louder and remained on the branch. "Well, I know you aren't Shadow. I told him to go away." Oh, great, now he had her talking to birds. She decided to ignore it, and turned her back on it.

Just as she turned away, a shadow from above darkened everything around her. Gasping, she realized a dragon was landing beside her, or at least she thought it was a dragon. It was the ugliest one that she had ever seen. Gray and twisted, it looked malformed. It was hard for her to tear her gaze away from the actual dragon to look up at its rider, but when she did, she was shocked. Sitting on top of the dragon was a person whom she recognized and had never wanted to see again. She stepped away, and moved to run, when he spoke. "I wouldn't do that. You would lose your chance to bond."

"You… you," she seethed with every deep breath that she struggled to take in order to just muster those two words, and it was all she could say as she backed away. Seated behind him was Benjess, and he seemed perplexed that she should know the dragon-rider and consequently was so antagonistic.

"Why are you so angry? He is here to help you," Benjess asked.

"Well son, perhaps it is because I wasn't there enough for her. I did leave her quite often," Benjess had no idea what he was talking about. What did Courtnia have to do with his father? "I had to help you and your mom in the store sometimes for appearances. Also, I couldn't be with either of you all the time. I had other, more important duties to the master."

Courtnia shook her head, confused too now. *Who was he calling 'master' and why was he calling Benjess 'son'? Did that mean that Benjess was her…*

The dragon-rider continued, "At any rate, let me introduce you to your half-sister!" Benjess, perplexed, just stared at her.

She had lived in Lexonite a while now, but she had never met the person they referred to as Benjess' father… the man the villagers called Breker. He had never been there the few times that she had entered the herbalist's shop and this was not the name that she knew him by. This would explain why he could be so close to her all this time and she had never known.

Apparently the man that she had called father had this whole other family, and while she and her mom had been so poor that they barely had enough to eat, Benjess had lived well with a father and mother who owned the herbalist's shop. All those times that her father had disappeared, she had thought he was working, but now she understood. She had been thankful for his absences anyway because when he was there, he had only been violent and hurt them whenever he thought they said or did something wrong. She shook her head in disbelief, still shocked. Unknowingly, when they had run to escape him, they ran right to the place where he went when he disappeared all those times. *That figures. That would be my luck, and on top of that I came to Lexonite to bond, but didn't anyway.* Her father's hurting them was the biggest reason that she had always wanted to bond with a dragon… to protect herself and her mom, and now he was the one with a dragon. The man who was supposed to protect them, but instead was the biggest threat to them of all, now was even more dangerous.

"I'm not sure why you are shaking your head, daughter.

It isn't really that hard to understand, even for you," he chastised her.

"I don't want anything from you," she said as she backed away again. "Nothing that comes from you can be any good."

"Now, Courtnia, your half-brother stated that you wanted to bond with a dragon. Figures you failed at that too," Breker growled condescendingly. "But at least I can help you with it." He was climbing down off his dragon as he spoke. "The Lexonite council wouldn't even allow me to try the Primitus Challenge to bond with a dragon, so I found a way to do it myself. There is a man that helps those of us that can't do it when the know-it-all council thinks they are better than us and won't let us try. After all, who are *they* to say there is only one way to do it? I believe another young girl just bonded without their ridiculous challenges, right?" It was a rhetorical question. She knew that she didn't have to answer him.

"They let me. I did the Primitus Challenge, and I won," she whispered proudly.

"What? What was that you were saying? You really need to speak up Courtnia. You always were too silent as a child. If you won… where is your dragon? Winning their little game doesn't bond you, now does it?" Again, she knew he wasn't expecting an answer, but this time, she did speak.

"I was quiet as a child to avoid being hit by you, but now, I can fight, and I don't need a dragon to defeat you." She drew her whip. "Perhaps you would like to try to hit me now if you are brave enough to try without your dragon."

"That's what I like to see… a fighter. That's a daughter of which I can be proud. You sure are acting like my daughter now. Oh the bravery of the foolish. The master will like you." He laughed as he said it, and his dragon creature seemed to laugh also while he put his large head lower towards her, and with putrid breath breathed into her face. "That's just his way of warning you to behave. Don't worry, dear. We are here to help you after all."

"Now, are you going to mount my dragon, or do I have to help you?" The little bird above her was chirping like mad now. Why would it do that? She began to suspect that it was Shadow after all and worried for his safety because of the attention he was drawing with all the noise.

As she suspected and feared, the ugly gray dragon noticed it, and immediately snapped at it, but his head was too big to get through the trees where the bird perched, and thankfully, for some reason, it didn't pursue knocking the trees down to get at it. When Breker saw Courtnia watching, he figured out what she was thinking and told her, "Uh, it wouldn't do… to cause a lot of destruction or noise right here at the edge of the city. There are a lot of dragons near here, so I had to tell him to control himself. It is only a dumb bird after all… ridiculous."

Courtnia thought about whether she should call out to try to get help from someone in the village, but she knew there were no council members this far out at this time of the day, and she worried that if the little bird was Shadow, Breker's dragon could harm him, so she decided that she should go with them. Also, if she admitted it to herself, a little part of her also wondered who this man was that Breker said could help people to bond with a dragon.

Benjess had climbed down and Breker walked over to speak privately to him, whispering something in his ear that she could not hear. Then, Breker turned towards her and said, "There will be plenty of time for you to get to know your half-brother later. Right now, he needs to go back to our shop. He has a job to do there." Benjess just looked at her and shrugged. Then, he turned and walked away, leaving her alone with Breker and his dragon.

Although they didn't know it, they did not leave her completely alone. As Breker spoke to Benjess, Courtnia felt something crawl into her pocket. Reluctantly, she followed Breker to his dragon and climbed on, but she was comforted to know that she was not completely alone. She suspected that she hadn't truly been alone once since she and Shadow had bonded. She had told him to go away, but thankfully, he had not listened, and had only waited for her acceptance.

26

When Hopel woke the next day, Candade was gone. Aggravated to no end, he groaned and using mind-speak, called out to Little One. *Well, my friend, it seems we are going to have to look for her again. She seems determined not to accept any help.*

Not necessary. I've been tracking her since she awoke and slipped out of camp. I figured it would be less work than hunting for her. I'll stop her and guide you here with my thoughts. Little One spoke to him even as she glided down to where Candade hiked. It was a little more spacious since the trees were sparser here.

Landing in front of her, she growled a warning for Candade to stop.

Candade sighed as Little One landed. She wasn't surprised to see her though. "Little One, well that didn't take you long. I was hoping you both would return to Lexonite. I can't risk you guys getting captured by Sanchezo. I don't want what he did to Swish and I to happen to you. If he captures you, he will try to turn you both. This is not your fight. That is why I left. Please let me go," she pleaded.

Little One growled a response. Candade wouldn't be able to talk to her because she wasn't bonded with her, but there was no mistaking her answer. As Candade tried to walk further, Little One gently nudged her back.

"Okay, fine. I might as well rest while we wait for him," she acquiesced and sat down on the ground.

It wasn't long until Hopel reached them since she hadn't gotten far before he woke too. Angry that he had to walk and waste time needlessly, his patience with her was wearing thin. "What did you think you were doing?" This is getting a little tiring. It is as much our responsibility to help Swish as it is yours, since we didn't report this to the council. And there is no way that we could let you go alone and return to face our friends and villagers if we lost you both!"

"I already told Little One. I just don't want you guys to get hurt or worse, captured, because of me."

"Well, if you are determined to do this without help from the council, then we will have to risk it won't we… because you aren't going alone," his tone gave her no room for argument, and besides she was already tired from so many battles.

She reached down to make a fire for them to have a bite to eat since she knew he had probably left without breakfast too. Reaching into her bag, she pulled out the herbs that Benjess had given her to brew in a tea.

"What is that?" Hopel asked.

"It is just herbs that Benjess gave me to help my nerves," she answered.

"Oh yeah, Lea was telling me about that. Let me have them," he reached for the herbs. Looking at him strangely, she almost didn't give the herbs to him; instead, she clutched them tightly to herself. When she saw that he wasn't backing down, his hand still outstretched, she sighed reluctantly and decided it couldn't hurt to let him see them.

"What are you doing?" she protested when he held them up for Little One to see too.

Using mind-speak, Hopel told Little One what he was

thinking. Little One could use her keener sense of smelling to discern them.

"I don't trust that herbalist, and you don't need these. You are one of the strongest people that I know. You just have to believe in yourself again… and the Creator's help… because you certainly haven't been yourself lately," he answered her just as Little One started hacking and sneezing. Hopel wasn't sure what the dragon was doing since he had never seen it before.

It is Fawgfoci, a herb that destroys focus and would make it hard for me to stay connected to you if you were to take it. Plus, we dragons are highly allergic to it. I thought I smelled something odd on her. Thank the Creator that she was keeping the bag sealed. I'm surprised that Swish hadn't warned her. Yes, it may make you relax, but it would also make it hard for you to concentrate on our connection.

Hopel told Candade what Little One had said.

Candade gasped when he told her. "Swish didn't even know I was taking it. I got it the first time when he was out hunting, and I kept it at home. I'm going to kill Benjess when I get back," she seethed. "He had to know what it would do, and he didn't even care."

"Well, see… you are definitely not thinking correctly because where would that get you? You can report him and let the council handle him by law."

"As if that would do any good. You said yourself that the stuff also helps you relax. Obviously, he is a good liar. He will just say that he gave me what I asked for," she began to cry now. This was not something that she usually did, but it was beginning to hit her now that it was all her fault. Taking the herbs that he gave her for pain and to relax is what had begun the whole process of weakening her bond and losing Swish. If she had just gone back to the healers instead of the herbalist, none of this would have happened. If she just hadn't taken the herbs at all, Sanchezo wouldn't have been able to use the stone to draw him away. "It was all my fault," she repeated over and over.

"Candade, you have to pull yourself together. You didn't know. Once your mind is cleared of this stuff, we have a better chance of getting Swish back, and that will give us a better chance to fight Sanchezo. We will have two dragons to fight his one dragon," Hopel tried to encourage her.

"What about his magic? It is stronger than both our dragons together." The next words that she spoke were even more difficult to get out between sobs. "What about if it is too late, and I can't reach him?"

"You can't think like that. He tried to break your bond before and couldn't. That is why he used the herbs and even then I don't think he believed it would work since he tried to kill you, and look, it didn't work. I don't know why Benjess is helping him, but when we get back we will find out, believe me." Hopel reached down for her hand and pulled her up. "We need to eat first, and we will walk a little before flying to give your mind time to be cleared of the drugs. How long has it been since you took them?"

"I usually brew tea in the morning and the evening, but I didn't do it last eve. After the battle that we had, I was so exhausted that I just went to sleep without it. Likewise, this morning I just wanted to sneak away to protect you and Little One, so I didn't make any tea today yet either," she was no longer crying and spoke more clearly, looking back and forth between Hopel and Little One, who seem to be mind-speaking back and forth at the same time. With all three of them strategizing on what to do next, she was able to regain her composure.

"Okay, Little One says it should only take a few days to pass out of your system. Yesterday, plus the two it will take to get to the cave should do it. We will take our time just in case," he told her.

He decided that before they left, they would both take

some time to practice sparring too. Candade was probably out of practice, and he could use some too if they were to survive the next thing Sanchezo threw at them. For some reason, he seemed to want Candade dead this time. That didn't make sense to him because he thought he needed her to join him to control Swish. Perhaps he didn't need her anymore with the stone. Perhaps the dragon stone controlled Swish already now. That thought worried him.

If nothing else, sparring would help them work off some nervous energy and build her immunity up again.

27

Courtnia didn't know where they were. They rested on some tall mountain peak. Breker had told her that it took more than one day to reach their destination. She dreaded having to spend more time with him. Indeed, she regretted this whole decision. She contemplated using the double-edged blade at the end of her whip to slice him through when he slept, but ultimately she knew that she wouldn't be able to kill him. Despite how he had beat and treated them, he was still her father. Killing him wasn't an option. Deep down inside of her, she believed that everyone needed the chance to change, and deep down inside of her because he was still her father, she hoped he would. Killing could only happen to protect one's self and others. So, how would she escape? How indeed? There was no way off this mountain cliff unless she flew. The ugly dragon creature could also catch her fairly easily.

"I know what you are thinking," Breker spoke, but never turned around from where he was lying on his side facing away from her. "I'm not sure why you are contemplating it though. We are only trying to give you what you want. You are my daughter after all. I'm just trying to help you."

"I doubt that. You never did a thing that didn't benefit you somehow," she hissed.

"Such ambivalence from my own blood. I suggest you rest. We have a long day of flying tomorrow."

"Can you at least tell me where we are going?"

"We are going to see a man named Sanchezo, my master," he answered.

Courtnia drew in her breath. She had heard of him before, and it wasn't good.

Ignoring her gasp, he continued. "He lost his bonded dragon once, and it grieved him so much that he searched for a way to bond again without those ridiculous rules of letting the dragon choose freely after proving yourself worthy." She could have sworn that his dragon creature's body twitched when he said those words. "We know they never choose a person twice. Finally, he found a way that worked, but rather than be happy for him, the council shunned him. Really, no matter what you heard, it isn't his fault. It is the Lexonite council that tried to keep him from bonding the way they tried to keep me from bonding. They are the ones that are evil, not my master. He only wants to help others to form bonds with a dragon. How could he be as bad as you heard when that is his goal?" It sounded legitimate, but Courtnia knew it was deception… twisted truth to make her believe… that is what the demons did… they would use just enough truth to trick you into believing the evil they wanted you to do.

"What… what if I change my mind?" What if I no longer want to bond with a dragon?" She spoke quickly.

"Uh, it's a little too late for that. Again, I suggest you go to sleep. We have a long day tomorrow. I especially suggest when we get there that you don't embarrass me in front of the master with that kind of nonsense talk… because if you do, you will be sorry." This time, he didn't try to feign kindness and the threat in his voice was obvious. It reminded her of the many times as a child that he had hurt her when she didn't do what he thought that she should.

She reached into her pocket. She thought the creature that had climbed in there was a lizard, but now it was a ball of fur. He had changed into some animal that was small enough to hide in her pocket, but with a fur coat that would keep him warm on these peaks. Courtnia pulled her own coat around her. She hadn't dressed warmly enough because she'd had no idea where they would be going. The fire that his dragon creature had helped him build was barely keeping her warm enough. She doubted that she would sleep even if her racing mind would allow her to do so. She didn't have his dragon for warmth either. He didn't seem to care if she survived the night or not.

She turned her back completely on him then, staying as close to the fire as possible. She wasn't afraid that he would try to hurt her now. She knew he wouldn't have a problem going to sleep next to his warm dragon. After a hunt, his dragon creature was already deep in sleep too.

Thus, on the other side of the fire, her front side protected from their view, Shadow could venture out a little. He seemed to understand her thoughts, and climbing out of her pocket, he lay down in front of her and grew into the dog he originally had been when she first saw him, only a little smaller to avoid being seen. Lying as close to her as possible, he warmed her.

She felt as if he was trying to speak to her, but she still couldn't understand him. She knew that she should probably try harder to let him into her thoughts, but she still wasn't sure that she wanted this.

28

Nohm and Lisbeth were worried about Hopel and Candade. They still hadn't returned. Speaking now with Lea, they could barely believe Hopel's little sister's hair had changed to an icy white color that resembled her egg. They had never seen anything like it in any other dragon-rider.

"I still say we should go look for them," Lea pleaded with the other two, distraught that her brother hadn't come back with Candade.

"You know that we want to find them too, kiddo," Nohm worriedly answered her, "but there is no way that we could find them. Our dragons are babies in their eggs. We have to stay here for training, and we have to stay here and protect them while they are vulnerable."

"That Benjess probably knows something. I know he has something to do with this. I kept telling Candade she shouldn't go to his shop for herbs." Lea spouted angrily. Earlier, she had spotted him sneaking into the village. It looked like he had been out somewhere all night.

"That may be so, but we have no proof," Lisbeth spoke

up this time. "Going to him and causing trouble will not help us find them."

"I hate this, but I have to admit that this time, we are not going to be able to try to help our friends even if we could find them, which I doubt. This time there is nothing we can do but wait. Plus, we have to protect our dragon baby.

"There is one thing we can do… we can pray," Lisbeth emphasized.

"Yes, we can do that," Nohm answered.

29

Traveling for days on a dragon left Courtnia tired. She was uncomfortable having to ride so close to her father and constantly tried to move as far away as possible, but unfortunately that left her even more at a disadvantage for warmth. Also, his dragon smelled badly. She guessed it was because of whatever they had done to it because it really wasn't even a dragon anymore. Sanchezo and Breker had turned it into some kind of creature that resembled the magnificent dragon, but definitely wasn't, or maybe it just smelled of rotted meat from its hunt, but either way, it was unpleasant.

Below her, all she could see was whiteness. Apparently, they were in some northern place that held no life except a few snow-covered trees scattered sparsely around the mountain. She could barely see a few feet in front of them when they flew and she was unbearably cold. The chances of getting away grew even more unlikely, as if there was ever a chance before.

When she had awoken in the morn, Shadow had decreased in size again and was back in her pocket before anyone else had awakened. She had a twinge of conscience that she didn't try harder to communicate with him. Truly, he was dedicated to her because he was still with her even in this dangerous situation.

Why was she being so foolish? She spent her whole life saying that she didn't care what the other villagers thought of her, so then why was it so important that people knew that she had bonded? According to Xian, Shadow might be even more ancient than a dragon and even rarer... surely that should be all that matters! Without even knowing it, she must have opened up a little with that thought because she began to feel a tingling sensation in her mind, and she began to *feel* the words that came to her mind.

Feeling unworthy your whole life made you reject this gift. Plus it is pride. Those were the first words that she clearly heard. It was as if there was a scratching, or would she describe it more as a knock at the door of her mind...? Opening it and sending her the thoughts, the words. Within moments, she realized what voice was scratching at her thoughts. *Don't think less of yourself as did those village bullies who picked on you for your status or what they thought mattered, because your real status and the only one that matters is that you are a child of the Creator, but do, please, for all our sakes, think of yourself less.*

Don't think less of myself, but think of myself less? What does that even mean? Angrily, she couldn't help but respond using the connection she felt in her mind. She was irritated at his sarcastic tone that he relayed clearly, even if not spoken aloud.

For starters, stop being so full of yourself and stop blocking me!

Without even realizing it, she had answered the voice and that was when the voice had become clearer and louder. It was her bond. It was Shadow. She understood his thoughts clearly now as he had understood hers! His voice sounded deep and ancient, not at all like the chirping bird.

Finally, I have been trying to speak to you for ages, but you refused to open yourself up to hear me.

Was that chirping bird you?

Chirping? He seemed offended. *I hardly chirp. You just didn't listen.*

Okay, now who is being prideful? She let that sink in for a few minutes before continuing. *Well, why now? Why can I hear you now?*

I'm not sure, but I think you needed me more and accepted that you needed me. I think you were starting to realize that your own pride was blocking me. I know I certainly was trying to tell you that, but you weren't listening.

Uh, okay, I get it now. You don't have to keep saying it, and well, while all that self-growth is good and all, where does that get us now. We are in big trouble… thanks to me. She thought to him sheepishly.

There is no use worrying whose fault it is. We just have to find a solution. You never needed to bond with a dragon. I have been bonded to you for a long time. You just refused to hear me.

Why?

It was determined before us both. The Creator assigned me to you. That is all I know. I longed for you and found you, but you were blocking it.

The Creator? He cares that much about me?

Of course he does, but you were blocking him and me with all that anger. Thinking you had to bond to a dragon. Pffi. Now that you are open to our bond, it will continue to grow and deepen with a little work on both our parts, but right now we should think about how we are going to get out of this. I can get big, but I can't fight two dragons and dark magic.

Maybe I could jump off. You can change shape, fly down, and catch me, saving us both before you hit the ground, though even that won't help much when they can just swoop down and get to us.

That is a lot of risk, and like you said they can just swoop down and get us.

Can you change into something big that can fly fast, so we might outrun them? That little bird isn't going to hold me?

For your information, I can change into many other things and some of them might fly and might be big enough to hold you, but I doubt I could out run them and you are not ready to see more of me yet in other forms! I was hoping that by seeing me as the little bird, you would open yourself up. I was wrong. Really, I wasn't supposed to let you see me in another form before you accepted me, but I couldn't just let you die, now could I?.

Well, aren't you being a little cryptic? I thought we were opening up to each other. Besides, deep down, I think I already had accepted you. I mean deep down I knew it was you, and deep down I was grateful that you were there. I just hadn't admitted it to myself yet. Courtnia had never been so excited! Shadow truly was better than any dragon because he could change shape and become many things. Why had she been so blind? Why did she not realize that keeping his secret was nothing compared to what he would mean to her.

I just hope that it isn't too late now, he said when they both realized that Breker's dragon creature was flying lower and heading into the mouth of a cave. It was too late to try to escape now either way.

Oh no.

30

Candade and Hopel had been alternately flying and walking for days. They figured the exercise from walking was necessary for clearing the herbs out of Candade's system completely. They knew that they needed to get to the cave soon to help Swish, but they couldn't risk Candade not being able to communicate with him. They were hoping to get close to the cave where she could mind-speak and be clearer and louder with her thoughts. They were hoping that he could sneak out, so they never even had to go in.

What broke Sanchezo's spell last time though was when Candade and Swish were able to make eye contact and clearly see their love and bond, so who knew if it would work this time without the eye contact. They had no idea what kind of magic Sanchezo was even doing with the dragon stone. As far as Hopel knew, he shouldn't even be able to twist it and use it for evil. The stone was something that the Creator had given the dragon queen to help the world, but what the Creator had intended for good, Sanchezo manipulated and used for evil. Hopel had explained to Candade how he thought Sanchezo used the stone to warp the creatures that attacked them and apparently he was using it to hold Swish under some kind of spell. He told Candade what the council had explained regarding the stone.

How were they going to break the spell? Would they have to destroy the stone? Was that even possible? If they destroyed the stone, would that also destroy the light magic it was supposed to bring to the dragons and to the world? They did not have any answers, but they were nearing the cave now, so they guessed they would find out one way or the other.

Candade knew one thing. Her thoughts were already clearer. She no longer felt unworthy of her bond to her magnificent dragon. Yes, she had made a mistake when she took the herbs, but her only failure would be to regret the mistake forever and not push forward to do better. Sanchezo would like that… for her to give up and live in her past failures… to castrate her like a lion in a fight, so she would be useless to help others. She wouldn't do that though. She was human and she understood what had happened in her human frailties, but she was meant to keep trying and that was what she was going to do now. *Swish, I am getting closer. I love you and I am coming to save you.* These are the words that she kept saying in mind-speak over and over the closer they flew. Whether he was hearing her or not, she needed to keep trying to reach him.

31

Courtnia had already known a thousand times over since meeting up with Breker and Benjess that she had made the biggest mistake in her life, but when they entered the dark cave, she thought it would also be the last mistake in her life that she would ever make.

The cave reeked of death. The only way that she could describe it was there was an indescribable smell of decayed flesh. Looking around, she saw unrecognizable creatures that perhaps at one time had been normal animals, but now they were twisted and tortured beings. They scratched furiously at the cave walls as if trying to get to something though she saw nothing where they scratched. She shivered. *If we don't get out of this, I'm glad I finally recognized you, Shadow, and finally realized the gift that you are to me.*

She felt a sense of warmth emanate from him to her though there was no verbal reply from Shadow before Breker led them around a corner where she saw Sanchezo.

Even more terrifying than the cave, a black cloud of smoke seemed to be swirling in and around him, alternately appearing and disappearing. He spoke in a grating tone of voice, "Imagine my excitement when I heard you were coming, dearie. The daughter of my great nephew here." Sanchezo's smile was faker than fake and it didn't take a genius to figure that out, Courtnia thought. She looked at Breker, confused, and he just shrugged his shoulders. "So, let's not waste time since we know why you are here. There will be some requirements, but I do have the perfect dragon for you to bond with right over there."

"Requirements?" She stuttered as she slowly turned to look where he was pointing. The large beautiful dragon was staring at a stone, rocking slightly from side to side, and seemed oblivious to everything else. In her mind, she heard Shadow growl and felt his uneasiness. He was still safely hidden away in her pocket though.

"Well?" Sanchezo excitedly clapped his hands like an impatient lunatic.

"What's wrong with that dragon?" she finally mumbled aloud.

"Why… there is nothing wrong with him," he seemed shocked by her lack of enthusiasm. "In fact, I have a feeling that pretty soon, we are going to take care of the only thing holding him back… she has been a pesky thorn in my side for long enough."

"She? What are you talking about?" she asked.

"Shhhh… you speak when you are spoken to," Breker said as he swiped her on the head and knocked her to the ground.

Sanchezo smiled his oily smile again and with a greasy, grating voice that he thought soothing stated, "Oh dear, Breker, that is so unnecessary. I am more than happy to answer her questions," he said quite unconvincingly. "It is simple really. We are going to kill his current bond, so that he will be open to bonding with you… with a little added magic persuasion of course."

At that, she couldn't contain herself. "What? I didn't ask

for that! I don't want to bond that way. That is insane," Courtnia yelled.

Sanchezo mumbled some words and pointed at her. Courtnia regretfully knew something bad was coming before she even felt the pain emerge from her stomach. It was the worst pain that she had ever experienced. With a groan she fell to the floor. "I expect your cooperation, dearie. After all, it is you who came to me."

"Uh, yeah, my poor decision might have brought me here, and I have no one to blame but myself, but I did not sign up to bring harm to anyone else," she fought to stand up as she spoke these words through clenched teeth, and finally, determinedly, she did stand back up.

With that, Breker backhanded her again, and again she fell to the ground. Still, with just as much determination, she got back up. In her mind, she felt Shadow growling furiously. She knew that he was ready to fight for her to his death, and of course, she knew if there was no way out that they would both die before doing this horrible thing that Sanchezo required. She patted her pocket. *Not yet, my friend,* she thought to him. *It isn't time. There still might be an escape.*

This time when she arose, she grabbed her whip. "Try that again," she growled at Breker. "I don't want to hurt you, but I am no longer a little child with no way to protect myself."

Sanchezo laughed loudly. "Ooooh, you were right. She is a fiery one. This should be fun. I remind you, dearie, you chose this. *You* desperately wanted to bond. This of course is the only way for you now."

Courtnia could just imagine all the people who bought into the lie that there was only one way for happiness, and then sold their souls to a devil like this man to get it. "I changed my mind. There are other things that I thought I wanted too, but I'm not killing anyone to get them."

The thing is dearie, I have no use for you if you don't

bond. I can just as easily kill you too. As he said it, the black cloud swirled in and around him. Breker must have seen it too because he stepped further away, and Courtnia fell to the ground again, writhing in pain.

Hopel and Candade landed near the entrance of the cave. Hopel had explained to her how he and Little One had snuck in to it previously without being seen, and they would need to try this again. Candade hadn't stopped trying to reach Swish from the moment they neared the cave. She repeatedly sent the same message. *I am coming for you. I love you.* As of yet, she heard no reply.

One thing she was sure of… her mind was cleared of the fog it had been in. If they survived this, she had a certain herbalist to see when they returned.

Little One, I think you should wait out here. It would be easier for the two of us to sneak in without you. If Candade can reach Swish, we'll fly out on him and meet you. Or we will ask him to fly out alone as if to eat and then sneak back out on foot ourselves. Surely, they let Swish leave to eat.

I don't like it. I don't want to leave you in there alone, she protested.

If we need you, I'll call you. At least, I'm thankful now that we can't hear what someone else says to his or her dragon, so I can call you without Sanchezo hearing me.

Well, if we let you, then you can, but we almost never let anyone but our bonded hear our thoughts.

Really, you are just telling me this now?

There was no reason before.

Okay, well, can you open yourself up to Candade as well, but not Sanchezo? Then, if I'm saying something to you in mind-speak, she can hear it too. It would be better than us trying to whisper.

It doesn't work quite like that. Rather…

Uh, Little One, he interrupted her. *Do you think you could explain to me later how you do it? We are a little preoccupied right now.*

She grunted as if offended, but nodded. *You probably wouldn't understand anyway.*

Hopel just smiled. *Thanks.* He felt reassured that even at a time like this, Little One could poke fun at him.

With that, Hopel and Candade entered the cave. As soon as they were in a few yards, they began to hear talking. Hopel shrugged his shoulders and gestured, mouthing, "Who is it?" to Candade. She shrugged also in response. He wasn't expecting anyone but Sanchezo and Cordo to be here.

Moving closer they began to see who was talking to Sanchezo. As expected, he was there with his dragon, Cordo, but unexpected, and to their consternation, so was Breker, the herbalist! *Maybe that was the nephew that Sanchezo had said bonded*, the thought immediately popped into Candade's head. *It is a little too late now,* she realized, *but the herbs and torture must have really messed up my mind for me to think it was Hopel. He has done nothing but help me.*

They could both see the ugly dragon creature that Breker must have bonded to with Sanchezo's help! They were both obviously his servants now, hanging on to every word he spoke.

Hopel remembered how, in the fore year, another villager, Taylor, had wrongly bonded. He had killed Candade's brother, and Hopel's friend, Natter, so he could bond with a dragon regardless of the consequences. He could just imagine how this bonding happened with the help of dark magic, and he didn't want to imagine it. They were able to defeat Taylor and free the dragon in death, but for it to happen again. For another dragon's life to be ruined, Hopel felt sick to his stomach. Whose life did Breker take to make this ugly deal with the devil? Now they understood why Benjess was working against them too. He must have been helping his father who was serving Sanchezo. Then, his surprise deepened even more when he realized there was someone else in there with them… Courtnia! *Why was she here? Was she joining Sanchezo too? How could they possibly manage so many? It didn't look like she was helping him though as she was struggling to even stand up.*

He looked at Candade, but her eyes had already moved away from Sanchezo to find Swish. He was at the side of the cave, staring at the dragon stone, and his head was swaying from side to side.

Fight it… fight whatever dark magic that evil man is using. Candade pleaded to him in mind-speak, but Swish still did not respond.

Hopel knew they were in trouble. They were now close to Swish, but Candade still couldn't reach him. He didn't see any way to free Swish and escape too, and now apparently someone else was here who needed help.

32

Numerous young dragons flew over Lea's head as she hurriedly tried to explain herself to her mentor. She and Uria were at the training grounds with Lea's egg. Earlier, at her home, the egg had started glowing and Lea felt an intense urging to place her hand on the egg and whisper something she felt the queen was telling her to say. Instead, she resisted the pull. She was worried because if the queen baby inside the egg was asking Lea to help her do magic, she remembered Uria's orders to refrain from using their connection for it. Thus, rather than give into the urging, she had found Uria, who at the time only seemed mildly irritated at the interruption to the training she was currently doing with other students.

"Lea, help me to understand. You said that you felt her calling to you to place your hand on her? What did you hear exactly?" Uria asked her.

"I heard her telling me she is saying the wrong thing by saying fight the dark magic… whoever *she* is… I don't understand. My dragon baby asked me to place my hand on her while saying, "Tenebrae abiit… in nomine Creatoris, levitate reditum… we order the dark magic away in the name of the Creator. We ask the light to return." What does that even mean? What would it have to do with us?" she asked Uria.

"I'm not sure Lea, but there are battles between good and evil being waged all around us that we do not necessarily see. I imagine the dragon queens are fighting a battle for the Creator and for the light magic. Your baby dragon is a queen, and apparently, though still in the egg, is in whatever battle is being waged right now too, and because you are bonded, you have to be a part of it. Maybe we all do." Uria answered. "Yes, I think Azra and I will do this with you."

Then, with a slight nod of encouragement, Uria placed her hand on her dragon, Azra. "Go ahead, Lea, and do as she asks." The urging was so strong, that Uria's gentle nod was all the encouragement that she needed. Lea placed her hand on her dragon egg, and both of them said the words she felt called to say, "Tenebrae abiit… in nomine Creatoris, levitate reditum… we order the dark magic away in the name of the Creator. We ask the light to return."

33

Sanchezo clapped his hands in enthusiasm over and over again as if he was an excited child.

Courtnia couldn't help it. She just looked at him as if he was insane.

"Oh, don't look at me like that. She is here… the one that has been a thorn in my side for so long. Of course, I'm thrilled. You should be too. We will end her disobedience once and for all. Now, *you* can bond, and I will expect a better disposition from you."

Then his dragon, Cordo, making some chortling noise that she could only imagine was dragon laughter, flew off into a tunnel in the cave.

Courtnia shook her head. She glanced at Breker with a pleading look, but didn't think it would do any good. Even if he once cared about her, and she doubted that he ever did, he wouldn't fight Sanchezo now to save her. Besides, she wasn't sure if there was any decency left in him.

At the other end of the tunnel, Cordo had no trouble locating Hopel and Candade. Swooping in behind them, he growled a warning.

"You better come in," Sanchezo ordered them loudly from where he stood. "I don't think he has much patience."

They knew that they had no choice with Cordo behind them. Thus, they stood and walked in the direction of Sanchezo. When they appeared, he clapped again. "Oh great, I got two for the price of one. I wasn't expecting you, Hopel. Where is that dragon of yours?"

Candade, not caring if they tried to stop her, ran immediately over to Swish and wrapped her arms around him.

Seeing Candade's love for Swish. Courtnia immediately felt her own love for Shadow intensify. Standing up again, she cried out to Sanchezo before he reacted to Candade's sprint. "They belong to each other. He is not yours to give me. I don't want him. Leave them be."

As soon as the words left her mouth, Sanchezo turned around and mumbled something dark again. She felt a swish of air and was knocked to the ground once more, this time the pain was unbearable.

"Quiet. I will deal with you later," he told her.

Breker simply stared at her with a warning glance.

Looking at Candade, Sanchezo screamed. "You, I will not deal with any more! I am tired of you!" Sanchezo then mumbled something dark again, and this time it was Candade who fell to the ground. The dark cloud that swirled around him now flowed from him to her. Candade gasped, choking and unable to breath. Try as she might, she was unable to stand up again either. It was as if the cloud was fighting her, choking her, and holding her down.

"No!" Hopel screamed and raced towards Sanchezo, just as Breker grabbed him and held him back.

Candade wreathed in pain, gasping for breath. In her mind, she called out to Swish. *I need your help. You have to fight his dark magic.* Weak and writhing in pain, she couldn't stand.

Struggling, inch by inch, she crawled closer to Swish, stretching to touch at least his foot. As soon as she touched him, she felt a sensation, a whispering voice in her mind, a feeling in her soul. It was telling her that she was saying the wrong thing. Instead, it urged her to say aloud, *Tenebrae abiit… in nomine Creatoris, levitate reditum… we order the dark magic away in the name of the Creator. We ask the light to return.* Even in her agony, as she spoke the words, she knew they were correct. She might be imagining it, but she had to try. She had to believe. She moaned and in her next breath, she spoke again, "Swish, I can't hold on much longer, you have to come back to me," and then she spoke the words she was compelled to say once more, "Tenebrae abiit… in nomine Creatoris, levitate reditum."

At that moment, the light in the stone seemed to change. Light swirled around it, blazing like a fire and shooting up. The stone began to spin wildly, and then it no longer glowed an eerie red. From somewhere, she thought she heard Sanchezo screaming, "nooo".

Within seconds, the white light began to flow out of it again. Swish roared the loudest roar that Candade had ever heard as his head stopped shaking and he looked directly now at Candade.

My heart. She heard him! Then, with resolve, he jumped towards Sanchezo.

She knew because she felt it as deeply as one could feel that he intended to protect them both once and for all by trying to kill Sanchezo, and she was afraid for him because she also knew how strong Sanchezo's demon magic made him. When she realized that he wasn't even going to get close to Sanchezo, she grew even more afraid. In mid-air, Cordo attacked him.

Meanwhile Hopel, struggling to free himself from Breker's grasp, turned to see Little One flying fast into the tunnel at that exact moment. Hopel hadn't called her because he was too worried about her safety when he saw Cordo, but he guessed she figured that he was taking too long to sneak back out and knew that something had gone wrong. She didn't worry about herself when she decided to find them. She was a dragon and would fight alongside them even if it were to her death. There was time to admonish Hopel later for forgetting that.

Breker was distracted watching the fight between Swish and Cordo, which gave Hopel a second to react. He shoved him to the ground as he ran towards Sanchezo with his sword out. "No you don't," Breker yelled, trying to stand up to grab him only to trip over Courtnia's outstretched leg and fall back down.

Hopel noticed the help she gave and knew for sure then that she wasn't helping Sanchezo and Breker. She was on their side.

However, before Courtnia could do anything further to help Hopel, the dozens of tiny warped creatures that she had spotted earlier clawing the cave walls now came barging towards them, fangs dripping, and death in their eyes. She glanced at them and then at Hopel.

"He somehow used dark magic to change the northern animals into these creatures of darkness," Hopel yelled. She nodded in agreement as she pulled out her whip and gestured for him to keep going after Sanchezo. He was still trying to make his way towards Sanchezo, who was focused on the fight between his dragon and Swish. Hopel glanced back to see Little One now entangled with Breker's dragon. It had charged her when she entered the cave. She was definitely smaller, but she was smarter and at least in her right mind. Each dragon reached for the other dragon's weak spot on the neck. He prayed for her while he continued to fight the creatures that escaped Courtnia and were blocking him from reaching Sanchezo.

The mutated creatures' attack on Hopel intensified, and

he glanced back to see that Breker had knocked down Courtnia again. Thinking that she would stay down now and out of the way, Breker turned to watch the dragons fight.

With her father distracted, Courtnia jumped up again to help Hopel and also to protect herself from the encroaching creatures. As they neared, she started to swing her whip and slice the creatures in half. At the same time, she mind-spoke to her bond. *Uh, Shadow, I know you can't see what is going on out here while you are in my pocket, but we are getting busy out here trying to stay alive, so no one will see you change, and Little One needs your help. Now is the time to come out!*

About time! As he mind-spoke the words to her, Shadow jumped out of her pocket, and while everyone was distracted, he began transforming into the being she had seen at the dragon cliffs. He might be even bigger now though. He still looked like a strange sort of rhinoceros, only with a larger mouth, wings, and black armored scales on his sides. Proudly, she briefly had time to think about how he was big and strong enough to help Little One.

Unbeknownst to her, while she had been watching Shadow, a creature had crept up behind her. It must once have been a snow leopard, but it wasn't anymore. Now, it had multiple eyes and horns coming out of the loose skin that hung from its body. Out of all of the creatures, it was the most formidable, and she should have been paying attention. It was too late for her to even raise her whip.

She thought she was done when *slice*, a sword went right through the creature. *Breker? He saved her. Why?* She looked at him, puzzled.

"I'm not done with you yet, daughter," was all he said.

Of course, he still wanted something from her. And here she had thought that maybe a part of him did care and there was a chance for him after all.

Breker turned his back on her again then to watch the fight between the dragons. He was dismayed that if this new creature that just appeared came from Sanchezo, it was attacking the wrong dragon! Seeing that his dragon was outnumbered and was tiring, he decided it was time to leave. Neither he nor his dragon would die on this day for Sanchezo. He ran towards his dragon.

Courtnia didn't have time to worry about him though as she continued to fight off the debased creatures that still attacked.

Out of the corner of her eye, she saw that Hopel and Candade had both reached Sanchezo and were both fighting him. Somehow the magic that he was using against her had weakened, and Candade was able to help! Together, they might have a chance. It was as if they fought their whole lives together. Back to back, there was no room for him to advance, and he had hundreds of years of practice with a sword on them, but he was still unable to better them as they worked together to defeat him. However, in turn, they were unable to better him either. Even when they charged him at the same time, he was able to block it. *Oh, so he was still using magic too in order to make him faster*, she thought even in the midst of her own fight with the creatures. She had wondered why Sanchezo didn't use any more of his magic to just kill all of them, but now she knew. He was probably weakened because he had used too much of it already, not only on them, but also on all the creatures he perverted nature to create. Now, he was using what dark magic energy he had left to fight both of them at the same time. That remaining magic, along with the years of experience with the sword that he had over them, might mean their death… if they fought alone, but together they were stronger. She was glad though that he was weakened. If he used any more magic than what he was already using to fight Hopel and Candade, he and his dragon could die. It was too risky. So at least they had that.

With Breker now mounted, his dragon slowly backed towards the entrance of the cave while keeping his eyes on his adversaries in case they were to attack. Instead, seeing his retreat, Little One and Shadow rushed to help Swish fight Cordo who, twice the size of any of the rest of them, was steadily overpowering him.

Sanchezo glanced sideways to see Breker and his dragon retreating and screamed, "Traitor, coward!"

It was just enough of a distraction. In unison, both Hopel and Candade thrust their swords into him. Candade's sword found his heart at just the same time as Hopel's sword cut through his neck. It was almost as if they had planned this attack.

At the same time, Swish, Little One, and Shadow were able to overtake Cordo. With Sanchezo's death, and the combined effort of all three of them, Cordo was finally defeated. With the other two attacking Cordo at his side, Swish had found his neck and made the final blow.

As Sanchezo drew in his final breath, with an extreme blast of wind, everyone was knocked over. A black cloud of mist swooshed out of him and swirled above them as if looking for a target. Seeming to find one, it headed towards Breker and his dragon who were still backing out of the cave.

Breker's mouth was agape when it flew right into him. "Oh," is all he said. Then, as he and his dragon turned and flew out of the cave, they heard his strange laughter echoing through the tunnels until he was gone.

"Uh, well that can't be good," Hopel said aloud. Candade nodded in agreement, and Courtnia had tears in her eyes.

Courtnia had finally realized that hating him did no good. She had even finally hoped that he could be saved.

Breker was still her biological father. Now, seeing that mass of darkness fly into him, she doubted there was any chance for him even though she still hoped that there was. She knew that despite their past, she would do whatever she could to help him. After all, her mistakes almost cost her Shadow, and she was fortunate to have not made the worst mistake of all by rejecting him and accepting Sanchezo's evil plan. She realized that though Breker was never a father to her, she had always had one in the Creator. Yes, she believed in Him now. She had gotten too much help not to believe in Him. In fact, He had probably always been helping her and sent her Shadow, and she hadn't realized it. Since she was always looking at the thorns, she never saw the rose. When she got back, she would tell Lisbeth that she was right. Life is not always easy, but that doesn't mean that we aren't getting help during the tough times, and if we are always worried and angry about the parts that are tough, we will miss the good parts and what we can learn from both.

Looking around them, Hopel, Candade, and Courtnia were somber when they saw all of the destruction remaining in the cavern. All of the maligned and deformed creatures had collapsed and died when Sanchezo had died. Distorted, dead animals lay everywhere. *What a waste of life,* they thought.

Candade spoke then, "Well, at least now that he is dead, the northern lands can revive and the animals will return eventually."

"I hope so. I would like to believe that the dark magic is gone, but we all saw what happened," Courtnia replied.

"True, but that is a battle for another day. Today, we will be glad that we have won this one," she said, and they all nodded.

"Where is that creature that helped Little One? I thought he was one of Sanchezo's till he started helping her," Hopel was puzzled.

Since she had no idea, Candade just shook her head and looked at Courtnia who feigned ignorance, shrugged, and smiled. She patted her pocket where she knew Shadow had gone to hide again. It was their secret, and she was finally okay with that.

34

Courtnia was riding with Hopel back to the village to give Candade time alone with Swish. Before they got to Lexonite though, Little One told Hopel, *Swish just informed me that Candade plans on going to the herbalist's shop to look for Benjess before going to the council.*

Well, we better go with her to keep her from doing anything stupid. He needs to be brought to the council.

It didn't matter though. When they arrived at the herbalist's shop, Benjess was gone. It looked like he had rushed to leave too, as items were just thrown about the shop.

"I guess Breker beat us back," Courtnia told them. She didn't know if they had figured it out, but she never did tell them why Breker had saved her. She definitely wasn't sharing that Benjess was her half-brother. She knew that they wouldn't trust her if they knew that she was related to them even though they had no reason not to trust her because she didn't want anything to do with Breker or Benjess, besides wishing that they could be saved one day from dark magic. Still, she knew how people thought with prejudices before they had facts, and she wasn't quite willing to trust her new friends with the knowledge that might make them not trust her. Plus, it probably didn't help her case already that she was in the cave when they arrived. There would be plenty of time to explain everything about that mistake when they went to the council. She wasn't about to do it twice.

When they turned the dragon stone over to the council, the council decided to hold onto it until Lea's queen dragon was of age to decide what to do with it. They seemed relieved that Sanchezo and Cordo were finally dead, but were very worried when the young riders told them about how they thought they saw a shadow fly into Breker and about how Benjess had disappeared too. There was nothing that they could do about any of that now though, so they were told to go home and rest before they tried to see any of their friends. The council also ordered them to keep everything that happened between them. They were allowed to tell their friends about Sanchezo's and Cordo's death, but they were not allowed to tell them anything else until the council decided otherwise. This upset Hopel the most as he didn't keep secrets from Lisbeth and Nohm.

"Well at least we can talk to each other about what happened," Candade told Hopel and Courtnia. They had decided that they would forgive Courtnia for her part in Sanchezo's plan to kill Candade because she hadn't known that was his intention, and they forgave her simply because they remembered how badly they had wanted to bond too. They understood what she was going through. Plus, they saw how she had rejected bonding the wrong way with a dragon and fought beside them in the end against their adversary.

Of course, Courtnia knew that she held something

back from everyone because she didn't tell the council or her new friends about her relationship to Breker and Benjess, and she decided that she never would. It didn't matter. For now at least, they were gone, and she was safe. She also knew that she was unable to tell them about her bond with Shadow. The only other person that knew about that, as far as she knew, was Xian, and that is how it had to stay.

Saying her goodbyes to the other two, Courtnia returned home to get to know her bond better. Walking along, she couldn't help but notice the village children playing in the street. *That looks so normal. What we went through when I grew up wasn't normal. We should have loved being with our father; instead we tried like crazy to avoid the violence that came from him.*

She didn't realize it, but Shadow had understood her thoughts and said to her in mind-speak, *Don't start feeling sorry for yourself, or you won't continue to grow. That experience has brought you to these others. No one has the same experiences, and you just have to use what you learned from them, the good and the bad, to help others now… offer it to them in that way. I can't help but wonder if Sanchezo used lessons from whatever it was that hardened him to help others instead of for evil, what good he could have done instead of all the harm he caused.*

Hey, how did you read my thoughts? Not cool! Courtnia protested, hardly hearing his words because she was astounded that he could read her thoughts.

Well, our bond is different from a dragon bond. I can do a lot of things that they can't. I've been reading your thoughts for a long time now… since I decided to bond with you. You would have been more in tune with me too if you weren't blocking our bond at first. Once you learn how to do it, you can block me from reading your thoughts, but I don't know why you would ever want to do that. Shadow answered her.

Uh, maybe for a little thing called privacy, she answered him sternly. Then she asked Shadow, *Well, now that I can understand you and speak to you like this in our minds, when are you going to show me your true form?*

See that is what I am talking about. I already did show you my true form. You just weren't paying attention to the bond to see it. I'll do it again. Shadow transformed into the silver bird with gold tipped wings and flew out of her pocket.

Oh, no. Courtnia groaned. *That is what I thought. Really? A weak, little bird? Can I go back to wanting a dragon?*

Better watch it, or I'll peck out your eye, Shadow tittered as he tried to feign anger in his tiny bird form. She couldn't help but laugh… a bird chirping angrily just looked funny, and soon they were both laughing. He was right about one thing. Now that their bond deepened, Courtnia was able to distinguish his laugh from the chirping sound that she used to hear.

After his laughter had finally dwindled, Shadow continued to teach her about himself. *Besides, I get to rest the most in this form, but it only takes a little energy, and I can transform into so many other things. A dragon can't do that!*

Hmmm, Courtnia ignored his slightly superior tone to continue her queries. *Really? Can that rhinoceros thing fly or are those wings just for looks, because I really want to fly?*

Better not. If we fly, I think I'd just drop you because you don't appreciate me enough.

Courtnia noticed that he still didn't really answer her question about flying, but she let it go, and just gave him a funny look in response. She would know the answer to all of her questions soon enough. Now, she just wanted to enjoy his friendship.

Back and forth the jibes flew between the two newly-bonded friends.

If anyone else had looked at them, all they would think is that Courtnia had a new bird as a pet, because some quaint little bird seemed to be following her. They would also think that Courtnia was growing a little crazy since she seemed to be talking to it.

People would say that she grew stranger because she didn't bond with a dragon, but Courtnia knew, for the first time, she truly knew, that it didn't matter what people said. If the Creator was happy with her and her bond was happy with her that was all that mattered.

The End

ABOUT THE AUTHOR

C.N. Strauser is the author of The Lexonite Legacy: Dragon Chosen and the sequel, The Lexonite Legacy: The Dragon Stone, young adult fantasies about friends and dragons united in a fight for the welfare of both species.

Originally from a small town in Pennsylvania, C.N. graduated with a BSED from Mansfield University in Pennsylvania and graduated with an MSED from University of Texas at Brownsville. C.N. has previously worked as a college lecturer and as a teacher in a variety of public school settings.

C.N. enjoys reading, camping, hiking, fishing, swimming, and spending time with friends and family.

When asked about the experience that led to this book, C.N. stated the following:

I have often told my students and my son that reading turned my life around and it is true. From the earliest age, I loved to read, and I had a special affinity for fiction about friendships surrounding mysteries, dragons, and animals. This love of reading helped set me on my path to becoming a teacher and a writer, and for that, I will always be thankful.

Like my characters, I wanted to travel and have new experiences away from my "village" from early on in my life. My experiences, both good and bad, have helped me to write these stories. It is my hope that although this book is fiction, my message of never giving up, learning from trials, and relying on God for strength shines through.

I hope you look forward to seeing how my characters grow and change.

My thanks and prayers go out to my family and friends for their support while writing this book, and of course to all of you, my readers!

ALSO BY C. N. STRAUSER

The Lexonite Legacy: Dragon Chosen

www.ingramcontent.com/pod-product-compliance
Lightning Source LLC
LaVergne TN
LVHW090954080826
845145LV00003B/1002

* 9 7 8 1 9 1 2 6 8 0 5 4 2 *